# Hey Kitty

SHILPA SURAJ

Om Books International

First published in 2024 by

**Om Books International**

**Corporate & Editorial Office**
A-12, Sector 64, Noida 201 301
Uttar Pradesh, India
Phone: +91 120 477 4100
Email: editorial@ombooks.com
Website: www.ombooksinternational.com

**Sales Office**
107, Ansari Road, Darya Ganj,
New Delhi 110 002, India
Phone: +91 11 4000 9000
Email: sales@ombooks.com
Website: www.ombooks.com



ISBN: 978-93-63951-96-9

Printed in India

10 9 8 7 6 5 4 3 2 1

To Mishka,
My first baby...

# One

## Katya

I stared up at the huge board spanning the main gate.

St. Thomas High School. It was huge, impressive in the generational institutional kind of way, and I hated it. I hated every brick, every stone, every student, every teacher, every classroom, every… I was running out of time to count all the things I hated about it... Oh well, to sum it up – I hated everything!

"Move it!"

Someone shoved me out of the way and I stumbled forward. My backpack went flying and smacked the head of a boy standing further down the corridor.

"OUCH!"

I winced at the scream and hurried forward to pick up my stuff that was now lying all around the boy, who was rubbing the back of his head.

"I am so sorry." I scrambled around his feet trying to pick everything up.

The boy bent down to help, one hand still massaging the back of his head.

"What did you pack in that? Rocks?"

I flushed at his irritated question. My journal *was* quite heavy, but I refused to go anywhere without it. Journaling kept me sane. And right now, with everything going on in my life, sanity was all I aspired for.

"Samar, what are you doing?"

The drawled question had me stiffening. There she was. The bane of my existence. My new sister.

How did I manage to get a *new* sister? My father married her mother and we got stuck with each other. Easy peasy lemon squeazy.

Samar aka the boy I'd just attacked with my backpack shoved the last of my stuff at me and straightened, dusting his hands. My heart started beating an entirely different rhythm. He was hot. Ridiculously, disgustingly hot.

Misha, the sister I'd mentioned, stepped forward. She looped an arm through his and stared at me, one eyebrow raised in disdain. Oh! He was hers. My heart thudded to a stop. I clutched my backpack and stepped past them.

"Who is she?" I heard the question and paused, wondering what Misha would say.

"Nobody important," Her dismissive voice was slightly raised, ensuring I didn't miss what she was saying.

I stopped and turned. Misha might be a bully, but I wasn't a pushover either.

"Not important at all," I said, making sure my voice reached them. "Just the girl who lives with you, in your house. You know, your sister?"

"Stepsister," Misha hissed, as her grip on the hottie's arm tightened.

"This is just like Cinderella." One of Misha's sidekicks giggled.

Misha smiled.

My stomach did a swift flip at the sight of that smile. I'd learned the hard way that when Misha smiled, nothing good ever happened.

“Just like Cinderella.” She sniggered. “It’s fairly obvious who the ugly stepsister is though, isn’t it?”

I flushed. The barb had hit home. The school bell rang and the crowd around us dispersed as everyone headed to class, saving me from further humiliation.

I turned away from Misha and her boyfriend. I had to get to the administration block and finish the first day formalities of joining this hell – my new school.

***

“Katyayani Shankar.” The hatchet-faced supervisor in the administration block pulled out a file and stared at it, lips pursed. “All the documents are in order. You are in 10 C. Do you know your way there?”

I shook my head. *How would I know? Today is my first day.*

“Aditi!” I flinched at the sudden shout, my ears ringing. “Come here.”

A girl with short, curly hair stuck her head into the office room.

“Yes, Miss?”

“This is the new girl in your class 10 C. Take her with you.”

Aditi nodded and disappeared behind the doorframe. I, the excess baggage she was saddled with, followed slowly.

She was waiting outside the door, looking very put upon. “Come on,” she said, striding off down the corridor. I hurried behind. *If I lose sight of her, I might just get lost in this campus and never make it to the class.*

Hmm. That wasn’t a bad idea. My feet slowed down imperceptibly.

"Hurry up," Aditi frowned when she realised I was lagging behind. "I don't want to be late for Mr Kukkad's class."

I sped up obediently. Whoever this Mr Kukkad was, I didn't want to get in his bad books from day one itself.

Three corridors, endless doors and one open courtyard later, we finally reached 10 C. Aditi abandoned me at the door and scuttled to her seat. As I entered the crowded room, the last hope I'd been nurturing in my heart died a brutal death. She was in my class, after all.

Misha sat in one of the last desks, the hottie by her side. Her sidekicks seemed to have surrounded her even in class. They seemed to be giggling about something. My stomach cramped. That something was bound to be me.

There was no teacher in class so I took my time, looking around for an empty desk. There didn't seem to be any. Except for the one, with a bag on it, in the first row. Defeated, I walked up to the 'bagged' desk. A bored looking boy with floppy black hair and rimless glasses looked up at me.

"Can you move your bag?" I asked. "This is the only empty desk."

He shrugged and moved his bag, making space for me to sit. Just as I slid into my seat; a short, bald man with a ferocious frown walked into the room.

"Sit," he barked.

Nobody moved since they were all sitting anyway.

"You," he said pointing at me. "New girl. Name?"

"Katyayani Shankar." I struggled to keep my voice from shaking. I heard a snicker from the back that stiffened my spine further. I was not going to let the bully make this any worse than it already was.

The teacher stared at me for a fraction of a second longer and then turned to glare at the back rows where the whispers and giggles were getting notably louder.

Silence fell on the classroom. I could feel the back of my neck heat up with the weight of everyone's attention.

"You can all say hi to the new student during the recess," the teacher announced. "For now, all of you open page number one hundred and thirty in your chemistry textbooks."

"As if we're interested." The rude whisper was loud enough to be heard by everyone in the class.

The teacher glared. "Your marks are ample proof of your lack of interest, Misha. Unless you plan to spend another year in my classroom, I suggest you open the textbook now."

No one dared contradict him. But I knew, and so did everyone in the class that Misha had not been referring to her lack of interest in chemistry. Not in this moment at least.

# Two

## Misha

"So, that's your sister, huh?"

"She's not my sister," I snapped at Samar. His interest in Ms Goody Two Shoes was plummeting my mood even further.

"Alright, alright," he laughed, shoving his books into his snazzy blue backpack. "Stepsister."

"Step-pain-in-the-ass," I muttered, walking away from him.

"Oh, come on, Drama Queen." He sauntered along behind me as I stomped down the corridor. "She didn't seem so bad."

"She hit you on the head with her bag!" I shrieked. Several heads turned our way. A guy mimed falling over in shock. I ignored the idiot and stormed off, Samar still sauntering along behind me.

I spotted *her* at the end of the corridor, chatting with a teacher. Anger swept through me as I stared at her perfect uniform, her perfect face and her perfect hair. Her. Perfect. Hair. It was meticulously braided into a sleek, fish braid. There is only one person I know who gets a fish braid that perfectly.

My mother. *My* mother!

My own curly, frizzy hair was exploding in every which direction from my ponytail, mocking me. I didn't merit a fish braid this morning. All I got was a yelled 'brush your hair'!

I wanted to scream, but funny mime guy was still watching me and unlike the teacher's pet over there, I had a reputation to maintain.

She'd already taken over my home and my mother. I wasn't going to let her steal my school and friends too.

*Maybe I'll just chop her hair off while she sleeps. Or dye it green. Or even better, glue it to her pillow.*

"Are you okay?" Samar sounded worried. "You look weird."

"Weird?" I watched Katya carefully. She was moving away from the teacher and towards the water fountain, at the end of the corridor, to fill her water bottle.

"You're doing this weird smile-glare thing."

I glanced back to see Samar contort his face into a hideous expression.

"Is that supposed to be me?" I asked, walking backwards, my eyes on his now laughing face.

"I'm not as good as the mime boy," he gestured over to where the idiot still trailed us. "But yeah, that's what you looked like."

I kept walking backwards, my mind carefully tracking our movements. We should be getting closer. I spotted the doorway to 9 C coming up. It was right next to the water fountain. Perfect. Right about now...

I stumbled on cue. Samar put a hand out to help me but he was not fast enough. I collided with Katya with a solid smack that knocked some of the breath out of me. My hand hit her stomach and I heard the startled 'oof' as she fell over. My hip throbbed from where it hit the wall as I scrambled to get my balance and bounce back on my feet. It was all worth it though when I heard the clang of her bottle hitting the ground and her shriek.

I turned slowly, my fake apology dying on my lips as I took in the sight before me.

Katya had clearly overturned her open water bottle all over herself. Drenched, dripping and weepy, she was a sorry sight. Water dripped down her shirt and skirt and trailed down her legs to collect in her socks. And her braid … her glossy fish braid was frizzing all over the place in wet tangles.

Perfect.

"Misha, dinner!"

I ignored my mother and continued my conversation with Mallika, my best friend and partner in crime.

"Don't be ridiculous." Malu laughed on the other end of the line. "You can't dye her hair green."

"Don't our teachers always tell us to dream big and reach for the stars?" I grinned.

"Reach for the stars not the hair dye," Malu snorted, thrilled with her lame joke.

"MISHA!" My mother had appeared in the bedroom doorway, breathing fire.

"Got to go," I mumbled to Malu and hung up.

"Are you deaf?" my mother asked. Her polite smile was quite terrifying.

"Not that I know of." I shrugged. The two of us could play this game. I could be terrifyingly polite too.

Sushmita Banerjee aka Ma was not amused. She walked into my bedroom and slammed the door. The poster of Harry Styles on my wall crashed to the floor.

"Is this going to be one of those days?" she asked, the polite smile starting to transform into a grimace.

"One of what days?" I twirled a lock of hair around one finger, deliberately goading her.

"One of those days when you make life as difficult as possible for all of us? Isn't that your 'new thing'?" she asked, suddenly sounding tired.

"No, Ma. That would be your thing, not mine."

We stared at each other, battle lines drawn. It hadn't always been like this. My mother and I had been the best of friends 'once'. And now … I didn't know what we were, but we certainly were not friends.

Ever since she'd fallen in love with someone who wasn't my father, we'd been anything but friends. And neither of us was willing to wave the white flag of truce yet.

"If you're not down for dinner within the next ten minutes, you can go without food tonight," she said, tersely.

"Then, I guess I'll starve." I glared back, mutinously.

"Fine." She stormed out of the room, her back a stiff, straight line.

"Fine," I muttered to myself. There wasn't anyone left to talk to; I may as well talk to myself.

I threw myself back on the bed and dialled Samar. Talking to him always put me in a better mood.

# Three

## Katya

Aunty Sushmita came down the steps looking like she'd just fought a war and lost. I stared down at my rajma chawal and tried to pretend I wasn't at the table. It was hard to win a battle against Misha. She had an unerring aim when it came to targeting your sensitive spots.

"All okay?" Appa asked Aunty Sush as she sat down beside him. She was a pretty woman and as far as stepmothers are concerned, she was fairly decent. She wasn't mean, evil or prone to concocting poisoned apples, though she leaned more towards serving badly cooked rajma.

"As okay as it can be nowadays," she sighed while serving herself dinner.

"Misha is not joining us?"

She shrugged. "Your guess is as good as mine."

"Katya, why don't you see if you can get Misha to come down for dinner?" Appa turned to me.

I choked on a mouthful of white rice, the safest thing to eat in this house. You can't really mess up rice, can you? At least, not too badly. The mess in my mouth tasted weird. So maybe it was possible.

"Let Katya finish her dinner," thankfully Aunty Sush came to my rescue, her perceptive gaze taking in my red and very reluctant face.

She was much more aware of what went on in this house; definitely more than my clueless father. He believed that he had the perfect, blended family. Was he clueless or stupid? Or just naïve? I wondered now.

Surely, he couldn't have missed my eerie silences or Misha's explosive meltdowns? Or at least Aunty Sush's heavy sighs? I swear, sometimes I felt scared that her lungs would collapse with the weight of expelling all that air.

But my father, he sailed through it all with a blissful grin on his face. He was in love; in love with a woman who wasn't my mother. Who, in fact, was the complete opposite of what Amma had been. Was that what had attracted him to her?

I gagged at the thought. Or was it a bite of the salty rajma that brought out the reaction? Either way, I was done with dinner.

"May I be excused?" Both adults stared at me like I'd announced my intention to belly dance right there on the dining table.

"But you've barely eaten!" Aunty Sush exclaimed.

"I'm not very hungry," I lied, silently begging my stomach not to growl and let me down. "I think I might be getting my period."

My father turned bright red at that. Aunty Sush smiled. "Do you need anything? Medicines or pads?"

I shook my head and made my escape with a mumbled goodnight. I almost stepped out of the door when she spoke again.

"You didn't tell us how your first day at school was."

"It was fine."

"Did you make any friends, Kitty?" Her kind smile didn't register. Neither did my father's hopeful grin.

*Kitty*. She'd called me Kitty.

The betrayal was huge; it took my breath away. How could Appa tell her this? *How could he?* I could feel my ears burning and sweeping away my usual attempts to remain cordial and polite.

"Don't call me that." My voice was rough, raspy, and barely recognisable.

Aunty Sush looked startled. "Kitty? Your father said it was your pet name."

It was … or it had been when my mother was alive.

*How is my little Kitty Cat doing?*

My mother's voice echoed in my head. Tears burned at the back of my eyes as I fled from the room. The unconscious cruelty in their words was like a pointed spear passing through my heart.

Why did Aunty Sush have to try to be nice? Couldn't the woman just poison a bloody apple instead?

***

I wanted to scream. I wanted to weep. I wanted to puke.

Instead, I sat on my bed and stared at the wall. How long does it take for it to stop hurting? Ten days? Ten months? Ten years? Never?

"Katya?" Appa hovered at the threshold of my bedroom.

"Go away," I whispered.

"I'm sorry," he said, miserably. "I didn't realise it would be such a big deal. Sush wanted to bond with you and we were talking about you and Amma."

"Don't," I interrupted. "Just go away. Please?"

With one, last, miserable glance, he left. I continued staring at the wall. It didn't reveal any magical solutions to my twisted life. I wished Appa hadn't listened to me and left. I also wished he would come back. But he didn't.

A scuffling noise broke through my muddled thoughts. Misha was sneaking past my doorway, her hunched posture and black hoodie and tracks made her look like a stunted cat burglar.

“Going somewhere?”

She shrieked, the sound piercing my eardrums.

“Bloody hell.” I rubbed my ringing ears but it made no difference. The cat burglar was now scowling at me.

“Mind your own business, you loser.”

“Epic comeback,” I grinned. The urge to needle her was irresistible. “Going to meet your boyfriend?”

“No.” She glanced nervously over her shoulders. “I was going to get something to eat. I’m starving. What was for dinner?”

“Your mom made rajma.”

She blanched. “Okay. Never mind. I’m not hungry anymore. Goodnight.”

I sniggered.

For one small moment, we grinned at each other, united in our shared hunger and rajma torture.

And then she shrugged. “I have a chocolate bar in my room. I’ll just eat that.”

My stomach growled. I slapped a hand over it.

Misha smirked. “Goodnight.” She went back into her room and slammed the door shut without offering to share.

The moment was over.

With another sigh, I came back into my room. I suppose I should be grateful for small mercies. Both Appa and Aunty Sush had good jobs which meant we could afford to live in a

three-bedroom bungalow in Bangalore or Bengaluru as it is now called.

Misha and I were not forced to share a room. Thank God for that! The thought of being stuck inside a room with that witch was more than I could stomach.

I picked up my phone and opened my social media account. I spent half an hour scrolling aimlessly and cyber stalking my old friends in Coimbatore. I wanted to message them but what would I say?

*I miss you. I wish I could come back.*

I may not be cool, but I couldn't be that lame. Instead, I turned over, hugged a pillow close to my stomach, hoping to stop its continuous grumbles, and tried to sleep.

*Goodnight Kitty Cat. Amma loves you.*

This time I couldn't hold back my tears. I buried my face in the pillow and let them flow.

*I love you too, Amma. I love you too.*

# Four

## Misha

"Do you ever wonder what it's like to be an astronaut?"

I stared at Samar in surprise. The two of us were having lunch in the cafeteria; for once, without any of our friends. It was a rare enough occurrence given we were always surrounded by our gang of cronies. I enjoyed their company most of the time but this was nice too; one of those rare moments to enjoy each other's company. There was the added benefit of having most of the school watch us sitting side-by-side.

"Since when do you want to be an astronaut?" I asked, tossing my hair and smiling for the onlookers.

He grinned and reached over to tweak my nose affectionately. "I don't want to be one. I was just wondering what it is like. Where does their piss and crap go? Does it just float endlessly in space?"

"Eww." I scrunched up my face. "Gross. Instead of wondering what it's like to look at the stars and planets up close, you're wondering where their poop goes?"

He swallowed another forkful of noodles and shrugged, his mind clearly elsewhere. Just like that, his mood flipped. I'd been watching this happen again and again with Samar in the recent past. He'd be happy, cheerful and somewhat affectionate and then a moment later surly, broody and snarky.

I shifted uneasily. "What's wrong?" I murmured.

He looked over and forced a smile. "Nothing. Why?"

I let it drop. Maybe we could talk about it when we video called each other later that night. The school cafeteria wasn't the best place for personal conversations. We anyway had most of the school trying to eavesdrop.

"Do you want to go watch a movie this weekend?" I changed the subject with a bright smile.

He shook his head. "I'm going to my grandmother's place this weekend. I'll only be back on Sunday night."

*Oh.* Disappointed, I stared down at the soggy vegetable sandwich my mother had packed for me. What was I going to do with my weekend then? I was used to spending time with Samar and I certainly didn't want to be stuck at home with my weird, so-called family.

I snuck a look at the table in the corner. Katya sat alone, quiet and watchful. She wasn't eating her soggy sandwich either. Was she feeding her lunch to the stray dog near our house too? He looked rather plump nowadays.

"Want to go join your sister?" Samar asked, the sneer in his voice making me flush.

"Don't be silly," I said, defensively. "Why would I want to sit with *her*?"

I took a large bite of my sandwich and gagged. I lunged for my water bottle and washed down the vile taste from my mouth. I really wished my mother would stop cooking. Some day, she was going to land us all in hospital with food poisoning.

Katya was watching me from across the room, a small smile sitting pretty on her face. She lifted her sandwich and toasted me with it. I dropped my gaze back to the table. I didn't need shared solidarity with her. I didn't need anything to do with her. Rather, I wanted her to disappear from my life so things could go back to normal.

I shifted uneasily in my seat. Normal hadn't been that great either. So, what were my options? Tolerate the troll and her father or go back to the screaming hell that my life had been before?

"Misha," Samar said, his tone visibly irritated. I jerked out of my thoughts and stared at him. He had that annoyed look on his face that I had become all too familiar with, off late.

"Aren't you going to finish your lunch?" he asked, looking at my almost full sandwich.

"I can't," I grimaced. "It's awful. I'll throw up if I have to eat it." He sighed and shoved his box towards me. "You can finish my lunch."

I stared at his half-eaten noodles and dry chicken. My stomach growled.

"That's not necessary," I protested, half-heartedly. "I'm really not hungry."

"Just eat it, Misha," he growled. "Everything doesn't have to be so dramatic."

My heart turned into a gooey, mushy puddle inside of me.

"Thank you." I linked my fingers with his under the table. "It's very sweet of you." He grunted, removed his hand from mine and took a swig of water.

Hurt, I turned to finish his lunch but my gaze caught on Katya's. It wasn't like she could have seen what had happened under the table but my cheeks flushed under her assessing, watchful eyes.

*I don't need Katya's pity. I don't need anyone's pity. I am Misha Banerjee. She still doesn't know what I am capable of.*

***

"Misha?"

Ma's voice stopped me on the stairs. I turned and eyed her warily. I wasn't in the mood for another sparring match.

"I came home early today because it's a Friday," she said. The false brightness of her smile almost blinded me. "I thought we'd go shopping. Just us girls."

Shopping? Just us? I stared at her, reluctant interest spiking in my belly. It's not like I had anything else to do and maybe we could order a burger while we were out. At least, I wouldn't have to eat home-cooked food for dinner.

"Sure," I nodded. "I'll just change and come."

Ma's smile changed into something more genuine. "Great. I saw this new boutique in Koramangala which looked really interesting. Some kind of fusion wear. We'll start there and then wander to whatever catches our interest."

I laughed and nodded. Her enthusiasm was contagious. I ran up the stairs and into my room to change into something more comfortable. Whenever Ma and I went on our shopping binges, there was a lot of walking involved. I pulled out a pair of soft blue capris and a white t-shirt with the words 'Make it happen' printed across it.

I changed as fast as possible and then went on a treasure hunt around my messy room looking for my sneakers. I finally found them jammed behind my study table. I was just lacing myself into them when the phone rang.

Samar!

I answered, the phone tucked between my shoulder and my ear. "Heylo."

"Hey babe," he drawled, his sleepy, sexy voice making me shiver. "What are you up to?"

"I'm going shopping with my mom," I said, a little breathless from trying to lace my shoes while juggling the phone.

"Yeah? Buying sexy bras?" he asked, that annoying smirk evident in his voice.

"Shut up," I muttered. Actually, that wasn't a bad idea. I did need new bras. My old ones were cutting into my skin. "I have to go now. I'll call you when we get back."

"Sure," he said, yawning. "Send me pictures of you trying on those bras."

"Ha-ha," I said, sarcastically. "Bye."

I hung up on him and left my room, the bedroom door slipping from my hand and slamming shut.

"Misha, don't bang doors," Ma's voice reached me up the stairs.

I grinned. Even Ma's constant sniping was not going to ruin my good mood. I was so looking forward to this shopping trip.

I jumped down the last few stairs and walked into the drawing room where Ma was waiting. It was only when I was several feet into the room that I realized that she wasn't alone. Katya was sitting across from her, looking very prim and proper in a pair of jeans and a t-shirt.

Fury erupted in my stomach but I kept my voice steady. "What is she doing here?"

Ma looked at me. "What do you mean?"

"Don't say she's coming with us," I warned, my teeth grinding against each other.

"Misha," Ma's voice grew brittle. "I told you we were going shopping. I told you it was going to be us girls."

MAKE IT HAPPEN

"You and me, us girls," I shouted. "When did she become a part of us girls?"

"Stop it," Ma snapped, standing up. "Your behaviour is unacceptable."

"Why don't you say what you truly mean? And that it's not my behaviour but me who is unacceptable to you?" I spat at her.

"Aunty," Katya intervened. "I don't really want to come. You both go ahead."

"Oh please." I turned on her. "Don't be the martyr. You've already ruined everything. I don't need you doing me any favours."

"No Katya." Ma's voice was steady and encased in steel. "You and I are definitely going shopping. Misha can stay home and think about how she has behaved."

The rage churning inside of me erupted like a gushing volcano.

"Fine. Go without me. I hope you and your new daughter have a great time."

I turned and stomped out of the room. I made it all the way to my bedroom before the tears started streaming down my face.

# Five

## Katya

I sneaked nervous glances at Aunty Sush's angry profile. She looked like she could strangle someone and right now I was the only one in the car with her. She pulled into the tiny parking slot outside a cute looking boutique and brought the car to a stop. She pulled the parking brake up with an angry jerk. I unbuckled my seat belt and opened my car door to step out. Beside me, Aunty Sush sighed. A tired, frustrated sigh that had me freezing.

"We can go back home," I ventured tentatively. "We don't have to go shopping. I don't really need anything."

"We are going shopping," Aunty Sush snapped even as her hands tightened around the steering wheel and she stared agitatedly out of the windscreen.

"Why is she like this Katya?" She turned abruptly towards me. "Is there something I don't know? Is she doing drugs? Or drinking alcohol? Or something else?"

"I – I – I don't know," I stammered.

It was actually the truth. I honestly didn't know anything about Misha. Mostly, we just stayed out of each other's way. Except for when she wanted to torment me. This was most of the time so maybe we didn't really stay out of each other's way. I cast a longing look at the boutique in front of us. If we were out shopping, we wouldn't be talking, at least not about Misha.

"I am so tired," Aunty Sush announced. "I've tried so many different ways to reach her but she just won't give me a chance."

I said nothing. I was trying to pretend I was a tiny speck of nothingness that didn't exist at this moment.

"You don't give Kannan such a hard time," she continued with her monologue. "You're always polite and respectful, well behaved and disciplined."

I sounded like a good pet, I thought resentfully. They were happy I didn't piddle on the carpet.

"I don't know what is wrong with that girl," Aunty Sush shook her head. "I don't know where I went wrong with her."

"Maybe you went wrong around the time you left her father for mine."

Appalled, I slapped my hands to my mouth as if it would help in taking back the words. Had I really said that out aloud?

The frozen look on her face told me I had. My father was surely going to kill me.

I opened the car door and shot out on to the dirty pavement. After a moment, Aunty Sush opened her door and joined me. We entered the boutique in silence.

I looked around the shop and immediately gravitated towards some graphic t-shirts they had on display. I prayed to all the Gods that Aunty Sush was not going to follow me.

A little while later, when I cast a covert look around, it was to see her staring at some artificial jewellery. I could have staked everything I had, which was really nothing, on the fact that she was looking at the jewellery but not really seeing it.

I grabbed a few t-shirts and headed to the tiny closet like trial room in the corner of the store. I tried them on but my heart wasn't fully in it. I changed back into my t-shirt and came out, handing over the t-shirts to the salesgirl waiting for me.

"It doesn't fit," I told her. "Thank you."

"Would you like to try this dress on?" Aunty Sush had snuck up on me. I turned towards her, stomach churning. She was holding out a pretty green and white floral dress with billowy sleeves and an A-line cut that usually looked good on me.

"I don't think..."

"Please Katya," she said, softly. "Try it for me."

My face flamed. I took the dress from her and went back into the pokey little trial room. The dress fit like a dream. As I looked at myself in the mirror, shame and guilt twisted in my stomach.

Aunty Sush had only ever tried to be nice to me. It wasn't her fault that I didn't fancy her taking Amma's place. After all, Amma would never come back. That, I think, was the biggest difference between Misha and me. Her father was still alive. She could have had her old, happy (or whatever it was) family. Except that Appa and I had arrived and changed the family dynamics completely.

I came out of the trial room and let Aunty Sush and the salesgirl ooh and ahh over me. I nodded when she asked me if I'd like to buy the dress. I pretended not to see Aunty Sush's pleased smile and slipped back into the trial room to change into my old clothes.

By the time I came out, the bill had been paid and the dress packed into a brown paper bag for us to take home.

"Thank you," I told Aunty Sush as we slid back into the car.

"My pleasure, entirely..." She buckled her seatbelt and turned to me. "Now which shop shall we go to next."

"Oh." I stared at her, flummoxed. "I think this dress is enough for me. It's already much more expensive than any other dress I have. I don't need anything else."

"Really?" she asked, looking startled. "Misha would never go home with just one dress. For that matter, she never buys anything from the first store she visits."

I flushed. "I don't really do a lot of shopping. It is mostly just the necessities."

Aunty Sush stared at me. "Well then, in that case there is no way we are going home. We are going to shop till we drop today."

***

Much later, as we sat in the food court of a mall and sipped on milkshakes, I stared at the shopping bags gathered on the floor around us. Till date, I had never spent that much money on myself in one evening. Dazed and drained, I continued to tally the haul in my head. I had an entirely new wardrobe; that too, a very fashionable one.

Aunty Sush had great taste and she didn't listen to my half-hearted protests. I now had enough clothes to last me for years. Excitement bubbled inside of me. I couldn't wait to get home and gloat over my new possessions in the privacy of my bedroom.

"Thank you," I beamed at her. "For all these wonderful things."

"You're most welcome," she beamed back. "I had fun."

I had had fun too. A sharp pang twisted my heart as I remembered Amma. It felt like I was betraying her memory by having fun with Aunty Sush. But then, Amma was gone and she was the last person who would have wanted me to be unhappy.

"I'm sorry for what I said in the car," I said, feeling rather ashamed of myself. "Amma would have wanted Appa to be happy and he is happy with you."

Aunty Sush didn't say anything for a very long time. She drew little circles in the condensation on her milkshake glass and avoided looking straight at me.

Finally, she heaved out another giant sigh and asked, "And are you happy, Katya?"

*Was I happy? No. Was I happy that my father was happy? I guess so.* At least that's what I told myself every day.

I shook my head, my eyes filling with tears. "I miss my home. I miss my friends. I miss my school and I really miss Amma."

She took my hand in hers and squeezed. "I'm so sorry baby. Your father and I..."-

I pulled my hand out of hers and dropped my head in my hands. The tears were flowing now.

"I don't want to hear about both of you," I sobbed. "It's enough that he's happy."

I told myself this every day. I repeated it to myself while I stood in front of the mirror, hoping that I could convince myself for a little longer.

"I was not in a happy marriage, Katya," she said, unwilling to let this awful conversation end. "I was miserable with Misha's father. And Kannan, he's been lonely for years. We found something special with each other. Something that brightened up the otherwise lonely future stretching ahead of us. We would never have taken this step if we hadn't believed it was worth it. You have to believe me."

"And what happens if one day you're miserable with Appa too?" I stared at her, tears streaming down my cheeks. "Will you just move on with someone else?"

She sank back in her chair like I'd slapped her.

"You were unhappy so you did this but Appa, my Appa? He never does anything wrong. He's always lecturing me about morals and principles and ethics? How did he do this? How did he let this happen? How did he have an affair?" I whispered the last word, my heart breaking.

"We fell in love," she said, her face stricken.

"And that makes it okay?" I asked, my heart feeling like it had been ripped into two. "At least Amma is never coming back but Misha's father is still alive. Still there. And you still did this. Maybe that's why she behaves the way she does. I don't understand either of you. I also don't know who my father is anymore. And I am not sure if I ever want to know you."

Suddenly, I didn't want the clothes anymore. I just wanted to go home. But where was home?

It was where this woman lived with my father. There was no escape either from her or her daughter. Not for a very long time.

# Six

## Misha

I stared at the blackboard blankly.

"Are you going to answer us today, Misha? Or next year when you're repeating this class?" Kukkad barked while facing the blackboard.

I flushed as someone in the front row snickered. Must be that mother stealing shopaholic I was forced to live with.

"I don't know the answer," I said, sullenly.

"Ashar!" Kukkad barked again. "Can you explain the answer to Misha?"

I tuned out as Ashar droned on with a detailed explanation that I couldn't have cared less about. Beside me, Samar reached out and squeezed my calf. It was meant to be reassuring, I supposed, but he scratched me with his bitten off jagged fingernails.

Wincing, I stayed on my feet until Ashar finally wound down and Kukkad allowed me to sit.

"Stupid fellow," Samar mumbled. Malu giggled on my other side. I rolled my eyes. If Samar told Malu to jump off a building, her only question would be 'when'...

I sighed. My best friend being in love with my boyfriend was not a complication I had time for right now.

Finally, the bell rang and we started packing our things. Since it was a Saturday, we'd only had half a day of school. This had been the last class for the day. I was grateful for the bell. I just wanted to get into bed and sleep for hours. The events of the previous evening coupled with my crying and yelling had left me with a heavy head.

Ma had tried knocking on my door once they'd gotten back but I'd made sure to lock the door so she couldn't barge into my room. Luckily, this morning's school run had been Uncle Kannan's turn so I didn't have to look at her or talk to her. However, there would be no escape at the dinner table later tonight or maybe I could just stay in bed for the rest of the day.

Knowing my mother, she would not refrain from torturing me further with another home-cooked dinner. *Please God, let it be Uncle Kannan's turn to cook today*, I prayed fervently. *Did Gods listen to girls like me? Especially the badly-behaved, hurtful ones!*

My head throbbed again and a vague nausea gripped my stomach. I shifted uneasily in my seat as I waited for the rest of the room to empty so I could head out too. Beside me, Samar and Malu were giggling and whispering about something. I wondered what it was but then decided I couldn't care less.

Finally, the rows in front of us emptied out and I stood up, slinging my backpack over my shoulders.

"See you guys on Monday," I mumbled.

"Hey Misha," Samar called out, hustling after me. "Wait for me."

"Why?" I asked, unable to keep the snark from my voice. "I thought you were busy."

He smiled, a smug little smirk. "Are you jealous?"

I blinked at him. "Were you trying to make me jealous? With Malu?"

I burst into laughter. The very thought was absurd.

Samar looked more than a little miffed as I giggled and snorted in front of him.

"I have to go," he said, giving me one last glare. "See you on Monday. I'm going to my grandparents' house this weekend."

I was still giggling too much to do anything other than wave weakly at him as he left.

"Why is it so funny?"

I turned to see Malu watching me with the strangest expression on her face. "What?" I asked, wiping the tears of laughter from my now wet cheeks.

"Why is the idea of being jealous of Samar and me so funny?" she asked, an angry tinge of colour sweeping up her cheeks.

I straightened, all laughter disappearing at the look on her face. "Because he's my boyfriend and I certainly don't think any guy would prefer you to me."

I knew it was hurtful and cruel, but it was necessary. If Malu thought she was going to take Samar away from me, she could forget it. He was mine. He was all I had left, the only person who still cared about me and I didn't care what minor problems we had been having lately, he was mine!

"Don't even think about it," I warned her, keeping my gaze steady on hers.

She stared back for a few minutes before nodding, her lips pressed into a thin line. "You're so paranoid," she said with a fake laugh, "as if I am dying to hook up with my best friend's boyfriend."

I laughed along with her, my laughter as forced as hers. "I knew you'd never do something like that. We're BFFs right?"

Someone snorted behind me. I turned around and stared at Katya who shook her head at the two of us, mouth twisted in a weird smile.

"More like frenemies," she said, brushing past me.

"As long as you're clear on where you stand with me," I told her, shoving back.

"I wouldn't turn my back on you," she said as she stumbled. "Awake or asleep."

I grinned even as my head pounded. "Glad we understand each other."

Katya didn't return my twisted smile. She turned her back on me and walked away with her slumped shoulders and drooping head. I wanted to throw my backpack at her head. Instead, I shouldered it and followed her out of the school, with Malu stepping beside me.

***

"I want to talk to you."

I groaned and buried my head in my pillow. I didn't have the energy for my mother and her issues right now.

"Why don't you go and talk to your new daughter?"

She slammed the bedroom door shut and came towards my bed.

"You will get out of that bed, sit up and have a respectful conversation with me," Ma said through gritted teeth.

"No, I won't," I said in a sing song voice as I kept my face buried in the pillow.

A second later the pillow was dragged out from under me and dumped on the floor. Ma flipped me over and made me sit up, handling me like a ragdoll. God, the woman was strong.

"Alright, alright, you win," I muttered.

She loosened her grip on me. I shrugged out of her grasp and looked at her.

"What do you want?" I made sure I sat as far away from her as the bed would allow.

"I want to talk to you." She folded her arms and stared down at her feet. "Then talk," I said, rudely, staring at my own feet.

"Do you resent the fact that I left your father? Is that why you are behaving like this?"

I turned to look at her, with an eyebrow raised, "What?"

"Because," she erupted. "I asked you Misha before I took this step. I asked you and you said you were fine with us getting a divorce."

I laughed. Was this some kind of a dumb joke? Was Ma drunk or something? "So, what do you want to know now?"

"Why are you being like this with me?"

Ma looked like she wanted to either hit me or cry. I hoped she took her time making up her mind. I didn't like either option.

"Misha, can you talk to me please?" She dropped her head in her hands. "I don't know what to do anymore. Just tell me what it is that I did or didn't do and I'll try to fix it."

"You asked me if I was okay with you divorcing Pa," I said, abruptly. "But you never bothered to even check with me about marrying your new husband."

She dropped her hands and stared at me. "I didn't care for the father I had. What made you think I would be ready for another one? Especially if he came with his own annoying pain in the ass."

"Misha, Kannan and I…"

"It's okay, Ma." I waved her off. "Pa and you had a horrible marriage, I agree. You had an affair and decided it meant more than anything else. So, you took what you wanted. Good for you. Just don't expect me to cheer you on."

"Misha…" I waved her off again. Her face tightened.

"Just don't get pissed when I take what I want too, okay? After all, I am only doing what you did." I shrugged and forced myself to look bored.

"Listen."

"Are we done talking?" I cut her off for the third time. "It's time for my video call with Samar."

"What's going on with you and that boy?" she asked, her face tense and angry.

"The same thing that went on with Kannan and you?" I batted my eyelashes at her for effect.

Her face froze as she grimaced in pain.

"Don't play games that you aren't old enough or mature enough to truly understand, Misha," she whispered. "The only person who will get hurt will be you."

"And you?" I asked, as I flopped back down on the bed and reached for my phone.

"And me," she agreed, sadly. I didn't bother looking at her while I dialled Samar. Weren't we done with this heart to heart already?

I waited till the door shut behind her before disconnecting the still ringing call and tossing my phone aside. I stared blankly at the empty wall in front of me.

Beside me, the phone started ringing. Samar was calling me back. I turned my back on it and shut my eyes. If only I could shut the world out too.

# Seven

## Katya

"Can we talk?"

Appa hovered at the threshold of my room. I nodded, warily. Through the open door, I could see Aunty Sush leave Misha's room. She looked defeated. There was no other word to describe her. But then, everyone knew that whoever took on Misha would be inevitably defeated.

Appa came in and sat down at the edge of my bed. He cleared his throat. "I hear you went shopping."

"Then you also know what else happened," I said, watching him closely.

He took a deep breath and nodded. "I'm sorry," he said, abruptly. "I was wrong. I have no excuse for it. I just..."

"Fell in love," I finished for him. "I know, Appa. She said the same thing."

"I know but that doesn't make it right," he said sadly, watching me.

I shrugged, "It doesn't matter anymore. Right, wrong, whatever ... it is what it is now."

"Do you think badly of me?" he asked, staring directly at me.

I shrugged. "You're my Appa and I love you."

"That's not what I asked you."

"Appa, please. I have a chemistry test to study for. I'm fine. You're fine. Everything's fine. Can I study now?"

I pulled out my chemistry textbook and picked up a pencil.

Appa took the hint and got up. He gently dropped a kiss on the top of my head and readied himself to leave.

I chewed on my pencil trying to keep the words bubbling inside of me from spilling out. I almost made it. His hand was on the doorknob when I lost the battle.

"Appa, was it just Amma then? Always do the right thing. Be kind. Don't be cruel. Be a good person. Put out good vibes. Make conscious decisions. All of these you constantly dinned into me ... was it only Amma who believed in these?"

Appa froze. When he finally turned to face me, he looked shattered. Like I'd taken a hammer and smashed his heart. It probably felt like I had.

"I'm sorry, Kitty," he said, ashen faced. "I guess I'm just human. Just like everyone else. I make mistakes too."

"So, you think this marriage is a mistake too?" I asked. I didn't know where these hurtful words were coming from but they were spilling out of me like some floodgate had been opened.

Appa shook his head, "No. No. I think I made a mistake falling in love with a married woman. But falling in love with Sush is one mistake I don't regret. I'm sorry if that hurts you."

I snorted, my new bitter avatar still very much in form.

"I love you Katya. I will always love you. Whatever else you might hold against me, please don't ever doubt that."

I didn't. I never would. That's what made it possible for me to go through the motions of this new life. I loved my father too. But I wondered if I'd ever known him. Or had he changed after Amma died. Was he a new person now and not the Appa I had grown up with?

"I don't," I told him finally. It was more to calm myself than him. I felt exhausted by all the drama in the last few days.

What would I gain from any of this? It was just easier to make peace with the situation and go with the flow.

Appa's face brightened. The hope on it was almost too much to bear. "I have to study now," I said, raising my chemistry textbook up so I didn't have to look at him anymore.

"Of course," he said, quietly. "Best of luck for your test."

The door shut behind him and I was left alone with my not so pleasant thoughts. I sighed and tried to concentrate on chemistry. The last thing I needed right now was to fail my exams like I was failing at life already.

***

"Your book has fallen on the floor, Katyayani."

I turned to find 'scruffy hair and glasses boy' or Ashar as the others called him, looking at me. "Thanks for letting me know." I bent down and picked it up. "My friends call me Katya," I said, pulling my pencil case and other books out of my backpack.

"I'm not your friend." My hands froze on my chemistry textbook. Was everyone in this school awful? Or did Misha infect them with her virus?

Before I could respond, Mr Kukkad came in and it was time for the test. He handed out the papers and took away our textbooks so we couldn't cheat. As if, we would dare try under his ferocious glare.

I stared at the questions on my chemistry test. I actually knew the answers. Imagine that! Whoa, beside me, Ashar was scribbling away frantically on his test paper. At the rate he was going, he would be done with his paper even before I began.

Mentally rolling my eyes, I started working on my own sheet. I was halfway through my paper when I heard Ashar put his hand up and ask for an extra sheet. *The show off!* On my other side, Aditi looked like she was about to have a nervous breakdown.

Another half an hour of tense scribbles and we were done. Ashar, of course, was done fifteen minutes before everyone else, extra sheets and all. Aditi looked like she was going to pass out. I wondered if I should actually fan her with my textbook.

"I'm going to fail," she muttered.

"No, you won't," I said, trying to sound all positive and cheery.

"Yes, I will," she said with a strangled moan.

I looked at her, alarmed. Was she really going to pass out?

"Do you want some water or something?" I whispered.

"Or something. You have any booze?" She eyed me like I had always been a clandestine bootlegger.

I reared back in my seat. "No, of course not. Why would I have alcohol? That too at school?"

"Don't shout," she hissed. "I don't need you getting us into trouble."

Ashar snickered behind me and I swung around to glare at him.

"What?" I demanded. "Are you telling me you have a secret stash of vodka in your bag?"

"Who has a secret stash of vodka?" Kukkad suddenly hovered above my seat.

The three of us froze. All around us the classroom chatter slowly died away. I'd always wondered at the expression, you could have heard a pin drop. Today, all you would have heard in 10 C was my thunderous heartbeat.

"I-I-I..." I couldn't get the words out.

"You-you-you?" Mr Kukkad mocked.

For the life of me, I couldn't get a full word or sentence out. And that's how the three of us ended up sitting outside the principal's office.

"This is all your fault," Aditi muttered, glaring at me. "Couldn't you keep your voice down?"

Ashar sat across from us in stony silence. He didn't even bother looking at me.

"This is not my fault," I retorted, sweat beading my brow. "You're the one who asked for alcohol."

Oh shit. We were going to get suspended or something. How was I going to explain this to Appa? He'd think I did it on purpose after our last conversation.

Far down the corridor, I could hear a lot of laughter and loud chatter. Misha and her buddies were making a point of looking at us and giggling.

I ignored them and concentrated on the mess I was in.

"Ashar." I turned to the statue in front of me. "You know what happened. You'll help me explain it to Princi right?"

The statue didn't budge nor did it answer.

Beside me, Aditi groaned. "I'm going to fail and get suspended, all in one day," she muttered.

"Would you shut up?" I snapped at her, "Your whining is not helping the situation."

"And you flapping around like a headless chicken is?" she snapped back.

A throat clearing had our heads snapping towards the Principal's door. The head of our institution stood there, looking at us over the rim of her glasses.

"Please follow me," she said, the words sounding like a death knell to my hopes.

The statue moved first. He walked ahead of us and into the Principal's office. He stood to one side and stared straight ahead. Aditi and I lined up next to him like hardcore convicts being held in police custody.

"So, what is this I hear about alcohol in the classroom?" Principal Meenakshi Verma looked at the three of us, her gaze flitting from two guilty faces to one stone face.

I raised my hand like I was in kindergarten and needed permission to speak. She looked at me and nodded. "Go ahead." I rattled off a confused, jumbled explanation of what had happened.

"There was no actual alcohol in the classroom," I rushed to assure her. "We were just talking."

"About alcohol," she said, her face stern and grave. "You're fifteen years old and discussing alcohol in school."

Beside me, Ashar sighed. *I'd just made things exponentially worse, hadn't I?*

"Ashar, I'm surprised at you," she said, turning towards the stone face. "I do believe this is the first time you've actually been sent to my office. Maybe these girls are a bad influence on you."

I snorted. I'd never been a bad influence in my life. I was somehow strangely proud to be labelled one now.

Ashar gave me a weird sideways glance but he didn't say anything, neither in his defense, nor in ours.

"Well." Principal Verma folded her hands. "For now, the three of you can go back to class. I will, of course, be speaking to your parents."

Ashar stiffened even more beside me.

"Go now." She made a shooing motion with her hands. The three of us turned and scooted as fast as we could. *No suspension. That was a good thing, right?*

"So, we're not getting suspended?" I asked as soon as we left the room, my gaze bouncing between Aditi and Ashar.

"Do you ever stop talking?" He finally spoke, even if it was just to snap at me. "That's a good thing, right?" I persisted. I liked having all the facts before I freaked out.

Aditi just marched off without uttering a word. I stared after her, outraged. She was the reason we were in this bloody mess. "Ashar." I put my hand on his arm. He shook me off.

"Could you please stay away from me?" he asked. "Change your seat or something?"

Stung, I took a step back. "Why should I change my seat? You change yours if you want to so badly."

"Believe me, if I could, I would," he muttered before stomping off.

I stood there alone in the corridor wondering what the hell I had done wrong and how I had ended up being the bad person. Not to mention the fact that the principal would be calling my father.

I gulped. Things were not looking up for me on any front.

# Eight

## Misha

"Everybody line up against the wall." I jogged on the spot as the others fell into place next to me. I loved going to the gym. I loved sports. I pretty much loved anything that kept me out of the classroom and away from books.

I noticed Katya take the spot as far from me as possible. Good. The more distance between us, the better. Although, after I'd overheard the discussion she had with her father, I wouldn't mind her being closer; just to rub her recent fall from grace in her face.

"We're going to have tryouts for the relay track team today." Coach Sebastian yelled to be heard across the large ground. "You'll be running in groups of five. Winners from each group will compete against each other till we get to the final four. After that we'll decide their position on the relay track."

Malu groaned beside me. I grinned. She hated sports. She'd rather be in the classroom painting her nails under the desk.

The boys were on the other end of the field, sitting in groups, waiting for their tryouts to start. I stretched, watching Samar watch me. He gave me his trademark smirk. I couldn't help flushing.

"On your mark," Coach yelled. I snapped my gaze away from Samar and got into position. I was in the first group.

"Get, set, go!" My mind blanked out as I ran. It had always been like this. Nothing could beat the joy that running gave me.

Coach blew his whistle as we crossed the finish line. "Good job, Misha. You win in this group. Come stand by me."

I went to stand near the coach, chest still heaving from the exertion. I noticed Samar watching, his gaze fixed on my chest, I turned away so he could only see my back. His increasing interest in my body hadn't exactly escaped my notice. I was attracted to him too but off late it felt as though all he wanted was to make out. And if I said no, then he would turn on me in increasingly painful ways.

Samar was easily the best-looking guy in school. And he was mine! We'd been together forever, in the beginning as friends and then as more. But now, things had turned strangely off balance for a while. But if I wasn't with Samar, then who was I? We ruled this school. He and I together, we were what mattered. I couldn't be alone. It wasn't enough. I wasn't enough. The next group ran and another girl, Vasundhara, came to stand next to me. The line grew longer as more students were selected; soon it was Katya's group that was lining up.

I didn't want to watch but it was hard for me to look away. Was she good at sports? I didn't know. I hadn't really bothered to find out. I didn't know much about her.

A few minutes later, I knew. She wasn't just good. She was very good; probably much better than me.

I wanted to scream but managed to stay silent as she came to stand at the end of the winner's line.

"Go and sit down girls. It's time for the boys to run now."

We sat down on the patch of ground the boys had vacated.

"Wow, Misha," Vasu chattered next to me. "Your sister is bloody fast. With her on our team, we might win the inter school tournaments."

I could not, I *would* not run on the same team as the witch who had ruined my life. My chest burned. Was I having a heart attack? I wondered if I should quit track. Would coach let me?

The first group of boys thundered past. Samar came last. I wasn't surprised. He was crap at sports. He was crap at studies too. To be honest, the only thing he wasn't crap at, was looking good. But he was my crap and I loved him. I grinned. That had been almost poetic.

Once the boys were done with their tryouts, we lined up for the final run which would decide our positions in the relay race. Vasundhara, Katya, Pooja, and me.

I wanted to tell coach I was feeling sick and skip the run. It wouldn't have been a lie. My stomach was actually churning. But my feet wouldn't move and my mouth wouldn't open.

Before I knew it, coach blew his whistle and we were running. My mind blanked out to everything else and I just ran. This time, it brought me no pleasure.

"Excellent." Coach Sebastian shouted as we crossed the finish line. "Over here."

We walked over to him, still panting and heaving.

"Katya, you came first so you'll be the finisher and be placed fourth in the relay. Misha, you were a close second so you're going to start the race for us and Pooja you'll be second and Vasundhara, third. Good job girls."

*Second. I came second*. The churning in my stomach got worse. I had come second to *her*. No way!

"Coach." I tried to get his attention but he was busy getting the boys to line up for their run.

"Misha." Katya came up to me. "Are you okay?"

"Come to gloat?" I asked her, pressing one hand against my stomach.

"Don't be stupid," she said, tersely. "You don't look good."

"Well, you never look good," I retorted. Yes, I know. Not my best attempt at a taunt but it was the best I could do at that moment.

Katya stared at me. "What is wrong with you? Why do you always talk like that?"

"Hey babe." Samar walked up to us before I could answer. "Want to walk back to class together?"

I did. I really did. I turned to tell him so but when I opened my mouth all that came out was... "Bleurrghh."

***

I had vomited on my boyfriend. I had vomited on my boyfriend in front of the entire class. I had vomited on –

The door to the infirmary opened and my mother walked in, cutting off my depressing train of thought.

"Misha." She rushed to stand by my bed. I pushed myself up and grabbed my bag which Malu had brought from the class and left with me.

"What happened?" Ma brushed my hair off my face and kissed my forehead. "Are you still feeling sick?"

I shoved her hand away and walked to the door. I didn't need her concern. I didn't need her attention. I didn't need her. She had her new family, didn't she? Why would she care if I was sick?

"Misha, talk to me." She kept her voice low so the attending nurse couldn't hear us. "Why did you throw up? You were fine when you left home this morning?"

I turned my head and stared at the wall.

"Should we go to the doctor?"

I shook my head.

"Mishti, please." My mother's voice was soft, the plea in it obvious.

"My name is Misha." I told the wall.

She didn't respond but her hurt and confused vibes crawled all over me making the churning start again. After a moment, she walked away from me. The vibes remained.

I heard her talking to the nurse and collecting the file on my puke incident. This was going to be my defining moment in this school. I'd spent the last six years cementing my place in the popular gang but starting today, I would be known as the 'Puke Girl'.

My mother came up to me and put a hand on my shoulder. "Are you ready to leave?"

I shoved her hand away and walked out. I didn't need her attempt at comforting me. Puke Girl was beyond comfort. Puke Girl was finished.

# Nine

## Katya

I sat in my place, wondering how Misha was. She'd looked really unwell earlier today. Would she bite my head off if I went to check on her? Should I still try?

Before I could jump up and go to the infirmary to check, our Math teacher, a scary old lady called Mrs Fernandez walked in and the class subsided into frozen quiet.

We were halfway through the period when Samar walked in. He looked freshly scrubbed and dressed in a set of school uniforms which someone in the administration department must have dug up for him from the lost and found bin. The pants ended a good two inches above his ankles making him look a little ridiculous; like they were a kind of mutant version of capris and trousers.

If Mrs Fernandez hadn't been glaring down her beaky nose at the class, there would have been a lot of giggling and laughing. As she was very much in position, we just sat in petrified silence.

Samar walked past my desk; a vague scent of puke trailed behind him. Apparently, he hadn't managed to get the smell off him completely. Or maybe, he just wasn't a very meticulous scrubber. He did look like someone who was a lazy bather. "I always said that guy stinks but this is new even for him."

I turned, startled, towards Ashar who was staring studiously at his book. Mrs Fernandez's gimlet gaze swung towards us.

"Something the two of you would like to share with the rest of the class?"

I just shook my head looking dumb. Ashar didn't look up from his book.

"Well then, if everyone is done admiring Samar's grand entry, let's get back to finding 'x' in problem no 56."

Samar's grand entry. I could feel his simmering, furious gaze burning into my back. Did he think I'd said something about him? Bloody Ashar. He was being an ass and I would have to pay the price for it. Again.

Class was barely over when Samar strolled up to me.

"Hey Katya." He was smiling but I had the strangest urge to run in the opposite direction.

"Want to join us for lunch?" Join them for lunch?? Was he serious? Misha would have *my* guts for lunch if I did.

I could sense Ashar staring at the two of us. I kept my back to him so he couldn't see my panicked reaction.

"Umm, I, I…" I stammered.

"Come on," Samar of the capri pants, said, "It will be fun."

"Misha won't like it," I said.

"Misha isn't here." He grinned. "Also, Misha isn't Mrs Fernandez." No, she wasn't. She was definitely scarier.

"Come on. It's just lunch," he coaxed.

"Okay." I nodded.

*"Stupid, stupid girl. What are you doing?"*

Stupid, stupid girl didn't answer. My inner voice had to talk to itself at thc moment.

I was too busy having lunch with the sharks of St. Thomas High School.

***

"So Katya," Vasundhara, my relay teammate asked. "Which city did you move from?"

"Coimbatore." I took an uneasy bite of my sandwich. The school cafeteria wasn't known for its food but this seemed halfway edible. It was still better than whatever Aunty Sush had packed for me today. Not wanting to eat it, I had brought some pocket money to school to buy myself a school lunch.

"Jeez, where is that village?" Samar asked.

"It's not a village." Had he failed in Geography? I was fast coming to realise that Samar's glossy exterior didn't have anything much on the inside to back it up. "It's a city, and that too quite a big one."

"Whatever." He leaned back in his seat and watched me eat my sandwich.

"How is Misha?" I asked him, more to remind myself of the witch's existence than anything else.

He shrugged, "Don't know."

Everyone heard the unspoken 'don't care' at the table as if he'd shouted it. Oh dear. This was not good. Suddenly, all I wanted was to finish my sandwich and disappear.

"So Katya," Vasundhara blurted out again. "How did you end up here?"

A deep sense of foreboding warned me not to say too much. This was Misha's turf. Her *Garden of Eden* and I didn't know what the serpent in it wanted. I certainly wasn't going to give in to its temptation.

"My father married her mother," I said, tersely. I put the rest of my uneaten sandwich on the tray and stood up. "I have to go. I have some paperwork to submit in the admin office."

"Don't be so boring, Ka-t-ya." Samar dragged the syllables out in a way that had me wanting to chuck the rest of my sandwich at him. The rest of the table stopped talking. Their heads swung between us like they were watching a tennis match.

And suddenly, I didn't feel like playing his game anymore. If I was going to play games, I'd rather do it on my own terms.

"I'm not boring, Sa-m-ar," I drawled. "I'm the interesting sister. The sad part is you haven't figured that out yet."

*Yo stupid. What the hell are you doing? Serpent alert!!*

Samar stared at me, the same smirky, sneery expression on his face. I was starting to think he wasn't capable of any expression other than that.

"Want to show me then? I can walk you to the admin department and you can show me how interesting you are."

The bloody creep was sneakily looking at my boobs. Suddenly, he wasn't even that good looking anymore.

A chair scraped back somewhere to my right. Ashar and his friend seemed to have finished their lunch and were clearing out their trays.

"Some other time. Ashar and I were supposed to do that together."

Samar stared. "Ashar? Loser Ashar?"

"My friend Ashar," I said, firmly. It almost felt like a million ants were crawling all over my body. Everyone at the table was dead silent now. There was some history here that I didn't know and I was right in the middle of whatever the mess was.

Samar burst out laughing.

"Yo Ash Mash!" he yelled. "Your *friend* here is waiting for you to go with her to the admin department."

Diagonally across us, Ashar had gone completely still. My face flamed. Any minute now he would announce to the entire cafeteria that he wasn't my friend and I could then die a hundred embarrassing deaths. Misha's vomit show would be forgotten and I would be the sister with the most humiliating moment.

But when he finally spoke, all he said was, "I've been waiting for her to finish her sandwich."

"Aww, true love," Samar mocked, the table full of his besties erupting in laughter around us.

"Ready?" Ashar asked, his voice steady. The hard undertone to it told me this was going to be a looong walk to the administration block. I had some explaining to do.

"Ashar and Katya sitting in a tree. K-I-S-S-I-N-G." Vasu sang as we walked away.

"Bloody idiots. How old are they? Five?" I muttered, savagely.

"I would think the idiot here is the one who gave them ammunition." Ashar didn't look at me as he marched out of the cafeteria. I followed, hurrying to keep up with his furious stride.

"I didn't mean to, alright? He was being an ass and I reacted and then I saw you and..."

"He's always an ass. The point is that you don't react. That way you don't draw more attention. And I don't care if you saw me. I am not here to rescue you. I am not here to help you." His eyes looked wild as he flailed his arms around and shouted at me. "And I am NOT your friend."

"Got it," I shouted back, my own volatile emotions bubbling over. "Message received."

All around us, students heading to their classes stopped to watch us scream at each other. In the distance, I saw a teacher walking towards us, a determined glint in her eye.

"There is no difference between you and him. None at all. You're as much of a bully as he is or any of them are."

I stepped away from him as the teacher got closer.

"The only difference is that," I added, nastily. "You're not as good looking as he is."

# Ten

## Misha

*@sxmar_69_ has posted a new story*

I stared at my beloved phone, my best friend. I'd pestered my mother for an IPhone because I was too cool for anything else. When I'd seen Katya with her OnePlus 6T, I'd taken great pleasure in flaunting it in front of her. It was hard to believe she didn't even seem to care or notice.

*@sxmar_69_ is live!*

He'd been very active on social media all evening but he hadn't had the time to message me. Were we over? Just because I'd thrown up on him? Shit, I'd thrown up on him. And, that too, in front of everyone. Not that I was going to let Samar dump me over something like that. I clicked on his account and Samar's face swam into view, talking animatedly.

*Hey guys. It's me, Sam. I've had the most epic day today. You will not believe what happened! True love's kiss, that's what…*

What was he talking about? Something twisted and painful crept through my body. Something was coming. Something I wasn't going to like. My stomach started cramping and churning again.

*I got thrown up on! That's right … no, no, not thrown over. Thrown up on. Right after our gym class. @misha_10_8 vomited all over me. Ewwwww, right? Sick!!*

Hot flushes ran through my body as I watched him imitate me gag and vomit on the screen.

*Guys, I can't get the stink off me. This freak has marked me for life. Any tips on how to get her off???*

As I watched, the likes and comments flowed in.

*Dude, did you get her pregnant? Why is she vomiting?*

*@misha_10_8 way to kill the romance*

*Epic bro! Dettol bath tonight. Oh man … if I was that girl, I'd just kill myself.*

I dropped my phone on the bed and buried my head in my hands. My phone buzzed continuously with people messaging, tagging and commenting. I couldn't bring myself to go through any of it.

How could he have done this? Samar had a huge social media and streaming video following. He was very popular and his audience, which mostly consisted of girls who were in love with him and boys who wanted to be like him, were quite rabid in their devotion to him. I'd always been very proud of his popularity. Now, I wanted to gag.

I glanced down at my phone screen as it buzzed again.

948 likes, 399 comments, 15 shares

*If I was that girl, I'd just kill myself.* The words buzzed in my head as my phone continued to vibrate next to me.

"Turn it off." Katya stood in the doorway looking at me, pity writ large in her eyes. "Turn the bloody phone off."

Something flared inside me. The little country mouse was pitying me! That's what my life had come to. That's what one bad day had brought me to. When I didn't move, she came into the room and turned the phone off herself. Tossing it back on the bed, she left without another word.

*If I was that girl, I'd just kill myself.*

Maybe I should.

***

It had gone viral. Someone had taken a picture of Samar immediately after I'd thrown up on him and uploaded that too. Everyone was taking great pleasure in my epic disaster.

I pulled out my phone. I'd developed a morbid new hobby. I checked how many new people trolled, hated, and viciously mocked me every half an hour. It looked like there were a lot of people sitting idle with a lot of free time.

I slid down in my bed and pulled the comforter over my head.

"Mishti, how are you feeling today?"

My mother had taken the day off to take care of me. This apparently involved hovering over me, checking my temperature every half an hour and feeding me curd rice with Uncle Kannan's homemade lime pickle.

Katya and Uncle Kannan had left for school and work respectively, so the house was otherwise quiet.

"Mishti?"

I realized I hadn't answered Ma as yet. I grunted in response. She didn't ask again nor did she pester me for an answer. It took me a moment to realise she hadn't left the room but was settling down near the foot of my bed with a book.

"What do you want?" I asked her abruptly. I wanted her gone so I could check my phone again. Maybe someone would have some more helpful suggestions like the 'kill yourself' person, I thought bitterly.

"I thought we could spend some quality time together." Ma smiled gently. "It's so rare for it to be just the two of us nowadays."

"And whose fault is that?"

The raised words lay between us. Sharp, deadly, pointed.

"Mishti." She laid a hand on my foot.

"Don't call me that." I jerked my leg away from her.

"Why not?" Ma stood, her face set.

"Because I'm not your Mishti anymore."

"Then who are you?" Her voice was calm even though her eyes were smarting with tears.

"Nobody that matters to you that's for sure," I retorted.

"I know that the divorce hurt you badly and then my marriage to Kannan."

"I don't want to talk about it." I interrupted, looking away from her. "I don't want to talk to you. We're done with this topic anyway."

She didn't say anything for a moment. After a moment, she started to talk with determined cheer.

"Both of you are averse to being called by your childhood nicknames. You don't want to be called Mishti and Katya doesn't want to be called Kitty."

Kitty? I wanted to laugh. What a ridiculous name. At least Mishti was slightly more respectable, I mused.

"She got so upset the other night when I called her that." Ma was still rambling on. "Kannan had mentioned that it was what her mother always called her and…"

"And you were trying to be her mother?" I cut in with a derisive sneer. "Sorry to break it to you, Ma, but it takes more than using the same nickname to take the place of someone's parent."

Hurt flashed across my mother's face and for a minute, shame and guilt streaked through me for causing it.

Ma stood up, her every movement stiff and awkward. “If you need anything, just call out. I’m at home all day.”

“I’m starting to feel nauseous again.” I made sure my voice sounded bored. “I want to sleep now.”

I lay down and closed my eyes, pulling the comforter over my head. Silence filled the room until a few minutes later, Ma left, pulling the door shut behind her.

I lay in the dark cocoon of my comforter, mind teeming with a million thoughts. Near my hip, the phone buzzed again.

I closed my eyes, breathing deeply. It didn’t help. The tears slipped through, trailing down my cheeks and soaking my pillowcase. Thank God for the dark. It turned out to be my saviour.

# Eleven

## Katya

"So," Appa said, glancing sideways at me.

I ignored his hopeful look and stared out of the car window. He was dropping me to school today as Aunty Sush was staying home with Misha.

I wasn't ready to forgive him yet for telling his new wife the nickname my mother had lovingly given me or for even having a new wife. I continued to stare out of the window with the hope that the ride would be over soon.

"Kitty, I'm sorry." He sighed. "I was just trying to help."

How exactly was this supposed to help? He'd decided to marry again. I hadn't stood in his way. I had supported him right through without a single tantrum or meltdown. Even when I realised that the wicked witch was going to be part of Aunty Sush's dowry.

I hadn't even told Appa of all the ways she made my life miserable because I wanted him to be happy. But wanting him to be happy did not mean replacing my mother. Nobody could replace my mother. And surely not Aunty Sush, it didn't matter how nice she was. Or how nice she tried to be.

"So," he said again when I didn't reply. "You're turning sixteen in a few days. Have you decided where you want to have your birthday party? You need to start preparing your guest list also?"

Was he joking? He couldn't possibly be this clueless, could he? "Are you trying to be funny?" I asked, furious at his idiotic question.

"Why would it be funny?" he asked, bewildered. We pulled up in front of the school gates. "Don't you want to invite all your friends and have a party?"

"I don't have any friends," I growled. "Ever since you decided to fall in love and drag me to a different city and dump me in a different school, I have been, officially, friendless."

I got out of the car and slammed the door shut behind me.

"Katya, wait!"

I ignored his hollers and walked into the school campus without looking back. I could not believe how out of sync with the world he was.

I was halfway to class when I snapped out of my outraged fury long enough to realise that people were looking at me and giggling. Well, they were giggling *and* whispering. My heart sank. Now what?

"Pukey didn't come to school today?"

My heart sank even further as Samar stepped in front of me blocking my entrance to the class.

"Misha didn't come to school today," I replied evenly. "She's still unwell. I would have thought you'd know that."

"And why would I know that?" he smirked, his flunkeys smirking in tandem behind him.

"Because you're her…" I stopped. Did I really want to finish that sentence? God knows what twist this creep would give to it. "I'm her?" he taunted, the others giggling in the background, the murmurs getting louder.

Ashar pushed passed us and into the classroom without a backward glance. I shoved Samar aside and followed. I didn't want to stand outside with a target painted on my chest.

Luckily, our chemistry teacher, Kukkad, arrived and even those jerks had to take their seats and shut up. If someone had told me I'd be feeling sorry for my evil stepsister, I would have laughed in their face. And yet, here I was.

I was struggling through polymers in organic chemistry when a white slip of paper appeared in front of me.

*A note?*

I stared at the inoffensive scrap of paper as it fluttered in the weak breeze from the creaking, overhead fan.

Where had it come from? Who'd slipped it onto my desk? I sneaked a look at Ashar who seemed totally absorbed scribbling in his notebook. On my right sat Aditi who'd pretended I hadn't existed since our alcohol disaster.

Who could have passed me the note? The boy who'd screamed that he wasn't my friend or the girl who completely ignored my existence?

The bell rang jerking me out of my daze. I grabbed the note and dropped it into my pocket before rushing out for lunch. I found a table in a quiet corner of the cafeteria and opened up my box with my drab, solitary jam sandwich. No cafeteria lunch today. Aunty Sush was determined we would eat home cooked food. Was someone going to tell her that adding processed jam to bread was not cooking?

I was just sliding my hand into my pocket for the note when someone sat down opposite me. Fair, tiny and with straight hair yanked into tight braids, the newcomer wasn't part of my usual set of tormentors. Was I now collecting new ones?

"Hi. I'm Bhavya," she said, sticking her hand out at me.

I eyed her hand warily before deciding to give her the benefit of the doubt.

"Hi, I'm…"

"Katyayani," she interrupted. "I know. Misha's unwanted sister."

Wow. Okay. That was quite a tag I'd accumulated.

#unwantedsister

"Want to be friends?" she asked, munching on a mouthful of noodles.

Friends? My fingers clenched around the note in my pocket. I was so desperate for a friend that my hands started trembling. And yet, I didn't understand this. Who was this girl and why did she want to be my friend?

Bhavya slurped her noodles and grinned. "You must be wondering who the hell I am and where did I appear from?"

I nodded. Words were a bit beyond me at the moment.

"I'm in 10 A, I managed to escape that bunch of vipers you call classmates. On the other hand, I endured them for two years, in grades 8 and 9. So, I have two years of torture over your two weeks."

She shrugged. "I honestly feel bad for you. At least, I only had to tolerate them during school hours. You're living with one of them. Also, just so we're clear on this, I hate Misha. I'm putting this out there because I cannot be friends with someone who likes her. It's not part of my life's philosophy."

"Your life's philosophy…" I'd finally found my voice. My fingers finally unclenched from their deathly grip on the paper.

"Yes." Bhavya nodded seriously. "I needed one to survive the bullying they put me through."

I smiled. "I'm going to need one of my own."

"Oh definitely," she said. "You're also going to need me."

Hope bubbled inside of me. A friend. I could finally have a friend. I wanted to throw myself into her arms, weeping and blubbering.

Instead, I said calmly, "My friends call me Katya."

"Well, Katya." Bhavya twirled more noodles onto her fork. "Welcome to St. Thomas."

***

"Katya kutty." Appa hovered by my bedroom door.

I put my phone down and looked at him. I'd spent the past hour exchanging messages with Bhavya on social media. She'd been updating me on all the different dynamics at St. Thomas while simultaneously introducing me to her friends. None of them were in my section but at least this meant I had someone to sit with during our lunch break.

The world was a considerably sunnier place than it had been this morning. Which meant I found it easier to forgive my anxious father.

"Not Katya Kitty?" I asked, smiling.

His tense shoulders relaxed. He slowly ventured into the room and came to sit beside me.

"I thought you didn't want to be called by that name."

"You know that that's not the case if it's you," I said. "I just don't want Aunty Sush using it."

He looked pained. "Katya…" he managed to utter.

"No, Appa, please. Listen to me." I sat up and hugged him. He hugged me back, his arms holding me tight. "I like Aunty Sush and I am happy that you are happy."

"But?" he asked, pressing his lips gently on my hair. His hand absentmindedly stroked my back.

"But she's not Amma and I don't want her to take her place. I won't be rude to her. I won't behave badly. I won't come between the two of you. But I can't pretend to have a relationship with her that doesn't exist. Can't she just be your wife without her trying to be my mother?"

"But Katya…"

"No Appa. I have you. You're my parent. I don't want or need another. Please Appa?"

"She'll feel let down and hurt," he said. "But if this is what you want, then this is what it will always be. Well, maybe someday you will feel differently and…"

I couldn't bring myself to destroy the lingering hope in his voice. So I decided to stay silent. The thought that the one who mothered Monster Misha could also mother me was mind boggling to say the least.

The phone beside me pinged again. My father saw me glancing towards it and smiled.

"I'll let you get back to whatever you were doing." He released me and readied himself to leave. He stopped at the door for a moment and turned back.

"You're sure you don't want to do anything special on your birthday?" he asked, both worry and hope shining on his face.

"Actually, I do." A sudden burst of inspiration had me bounding off the bed.

"You do?" My father beamed at me, coming into the room again. "Tell me what it is. Whatever it is that you want; tell me, we will do that. I can organize it."

"I want to go on a date."

He froze, his mouth hanging open.

"A d-d-date?"

I grinned. "Yes. You just said I could have whatever I want."

"You're turning sixteen," he whispered, looking defeated. "I wasn't ready for you to date for a few more years."

"How many more years?" I challenged.

"Another ten?" he asked, hopefully.

"Appa," I groaned. "You are so lame."

He sighed, squared his shoulders and stepped forward. "Okay. I'll allow it. But there are some rules."

"Rules?" I glared at him in mock affront.

"Yes, rules," he said, firmly. He was regaining fatherly ground. "I will drop you and pick you up from the venue. You will pay for the evening since it is your birthday. And…" he swallowed hard, "and yes, also no touching."

"No touching the food? The cutlery? The menu?" I was thoroughly enjoying myself.

"Each other," he growled.

"Fine," I sighed, dramatically. "I'll agree to all your rules."

He nodded, still looking frazzled. "Okay then."

"Okay then," I repeated, grinning widely.

With another nod in my direction, off he marched towards the door. Stopped, stared at the wall and then came back.

"Also, I need to know this boy's name so I can speak to his parents."

"You can't."

"Why not?" He dug his heels in, readying himself for an argument. "I need to know who you are going out with."

"You."

"What?" He stared at me, confused.

"You, Appa. I want to go on a date with you on my birthday. Just the two of us. And the last time I checked, thatha (grandpa in Tamil) and paati (grandma in Tamil) were not talking to you because you married Aunty Sush, so you can't talk to them about it."

"Me?" he asked, his eyes filling with tears. His arms circled around me in a tight hug. "You are the best daughter in the whole world," he murmured.

I hugged him back. "I know."

"Also, the worst for what you just put me through."

I laughed loudly. "I know that too Appa."

# Twelve

## Misha

My social media followers had dropped by 300 in one evening. Disgusted, I stared at my phone, disbelievingly. Overnight, I'd gone from being popular to being 'Pukey'.

Was this what my years of accumulating social clout had been worth? With just one moment of involuntary vomit?

My phone vibrated but I tossed it aside. Maybe I should just delete my social media account and create a new one. It would be easier than dealing with the legions of trolls that I seemed to have gathered.

I heard voices outside my door and walked over to listen. *Oh ick! It was Ma and Uncle Kannan cootchie cooing. Couldn't they do that in their room?*

I threw myself on the bed and buried my head in my pillow. What was I going to do? I couldn't be unpopular. I couldn't be the one who got ragged. I couldn't be … Katya.

I groaned. The witch must be loving this, I thought viciously. I hadn't been back to school since the 'Puke Gate' as I had taken to calling the incident but I was fairly sure of what was happening there. I was the latest joke. In my absence, both rumour and gossip must be floating around.

None of my friends were in touch except for Malu who made one embarrassed, hurried call to check on me. Samar wasn't responding to any of my messages, calls or voice notes. It was like I had ceased to exist.

My heart ached. Why did people stop loving me so easily? My father disappeared after Ma and he got a divorce. My boyfriend disappeared after I had one sick day around him.

At least, my father hadn't made a video mocking me and circulated it on social media. Although he had married again and had another child. A baby boy. A child he seemed to have a lot more time for.

Which was probably worse. I wiped my tears and sat up. I wasn't going to let Samar leave me too. I needed a plan. I needed a strategy. I needed my friends.

I picked up the phone and called Malu. It rang forever before she answered.

"Hello?"

"Hey," I said, as casually as possible. "What's up?"

"Nothing much. The usual." The reserve in her voice was like a brick wall, difficult to penetrate.

"How's school?" I walked over to the window and stared out at the traffic on the road.

"Fine." This conversation was like pulling teeth. It was obvious Malu, my best friend since kindergarten, didn't want to talk to me. "I should be back tomorrow." I made one last attempt to find our previous balance.

"Okay." She couldn't have cared less. It felt like someone was stabbing me in the heart. This hurt more than Samar's video for some reason.

"I guess we'll catch up tomorrow." I knew we would be doing nothing of that sort.

"Bye." She hung up before I could even respond.

Panic washed through me. What was I going to do? I had to do damage control. But how?

I heard Katya's voice outside my bedroom door. She seemed to be responding to something the parental duo had asked her.

I hated her. I'd hated her from the moment I got to know about her. I'd hated the thought of her and the reality of her had only lived up to my expectations.

A knock on my door jerked me out of my thoughts. I continued to stare out of my window hoping whoever it was would go away.

"Kukkad Sir asked me to give you these assignments. They have to be completed by tomorrow."

Oh. It was her. Kitty Cat. I swung around to see her putting the file down on my bed. A germ of an idea took root in my head.

"Let me know if you need any help." She backed away from the bed and rushed towards the door as though she couldn't get out of my room fast enough.

"Your help? No, thanks."

"Sure. Whatever." Katya left without a backward glance, the door slamming shut behind her. I sighed. The last thing I wanted to do was homework but I didn't want to be in trouble with the teachers, as well, at this point.

My phone pinged just as I reached my bed. Oh well, a notification on social media from Samar again. My heart started to thud rapidly. Homework forgotten, I sat down on the bed and thumbed my phone open.

A picture of Samar in ripped jeans and a plain black t-shirt flashed on screen. He looked gorgeous, as always. It was the caption beneath the picture that had my heart stop its rapid thudding.

*Have a hot date. Dinner at Mamagotos!*

He was going on a date? With whom? How could he go on a date? He was my boyfriend, wasn't he?

WASN'T HE??? He couldn't dump me after all these years without even having a proper conversation about it.

I started to type out a furious message to him but stopped. If I pushed Samar right now, I would lose him completely. The last thing I wanted was that. I'd loved him since Grade 6. I couldn't imagine my life without him.

I pulled out my homework sheets and sat down at my study table. I needed a strategy to get back on track with Samar and the only way to do that was to first get back on track myself.

No more moping. No more whining. No more Pukey. Misha Banerjee was back.

***

I stepped off the car the next morning, my back straight, eyes clear and bright. Behind me, I heard Katya saying goodbye to my mom whose turn it was to drop us to school. I didn't bother to wait for Katya or to respond to my mother's rather loud goodbye.

Samar was standing in a secluded corner of the playground, the usual gang gathered around him. They were gathered under the large mango tree that grew there.

I snuck into the nearest student's bathroom to make some cosmetic adjustments to my appearance.

I pulled out the stuffing for my bra that I'd prepared the night before. Once it was in position and my cups neatly fluffed up, I unbuttoned the top two buttons of my shirt to make the most of my new cleavage. Hitching my skirt up, I strapped my belt across the top so it showed way more leg than was otherwise allowed. I was going to have to fix all this before I went into class later.

I rubbed on another layer of cherry lip gloss and smacked my lips to even it out. I smudged my kajal a bit to make sure the subtle smokey eye makeup I'd applied was more evident. Loosening my braids, I pulled my wavy hair back into a sexy, messy bun. I took one last look at myself in the mirror and, satisfied with how I looked, left the bathroom.

I slowed my militant march down to a sexy strut, one that had most of the boys who were still wandering the corridors watching.

The group around Samar turned to watch me approach and it was only then that I saw who stood with him in the centre. Mallika.

The shock of seeing her with his arm around her shoulders was tempered by the fact that in the bottom of my heart, I'd already known. *Mamagotos was her favourite restaurant after all.*

She tossed her hair and stared at me as I walked up to them, with no remorse in sight. Samar had his usual smirk pasted on.

"Welcome back, Pukey."

I didn't know who'd said that and I didn't care. To my right, Mime Boy was pretending to gag and choke. I assumed the next step would be the actual throwing up bit.

I kept my eyes fixed on Samar. This little power game was between the two of us. Malu was just collateral damage.

I stopped in front of them. Malu put her arm around his waist and pulled him closer. Samar ignored her and continued to watch me, his lips quirked in that smug, knowing smile.

"Hey Misha," he said casually. Like nothing had happened and he hadn't been ignoring me for days. Like he hadn't made a public laughing stock of me and my one day of sickness. Like he didn't have his arm around my best friend.

"Samar," I smiled. I saw his eyes fall to my lips and then to my enhanced cleavage.

"Hi Misha." Mallika butted in from the side. "How are you feeling now? Not still nauseous I hope? Maybe we should get out of the way."

A round of laughter started up at the lame joke. I ignored her and the insinuation.

I pulled a sheaf of papers out of my bag and held it out to Samar. "I know you like me to help you with your math assignments, especially trigonometry. I copied out my assignment for you so you could refer to it in case you needed any help."

His eyes narrowed, flicking from the papers in my hand to my face.

"Take it." I smiled. "You know you want to."

The words were suggestive enough for him to smile back. He pulled his arm off Malu's shoulders and took the papers.

I didn't wait for him to thank me. I gave Mime Boy a casual shove with one arm toppling him into the mud puddle behind the group. While everyone was laughing at his sputtering and scrambling, I gave Samar one last glance, and turned and sauntered away without looking back.

I didn't need to look back to know he watched me walk away. The whole time. In the distance, I could see Katya watching us. I may have been mistaken but I was damn sure I saw respect in her eyes. I'd bloody well earned it, hadn't I?

# Thirteen

## Katya

I laughed. The witch was unbelievable. I hated to admit it but she'd owned that scene in the playground. I would have loved to see Kukkad's expression if he'd got a glimpse of Misha's femme fatale improvisation. But by the time she came into the classroom, she looked more her normal self, except for the scrubbed clean face and loosely braided hair. She walked up to the first row and stared at Aditi, who sat on my right.

"What?" Aditi asked, although her bravado was very shaky.

"Swap," demanded Misha, her body language languid and bored but layered with a vicious vibe. Aditi quivered a little. She gathered her stuff and started to move towards Misha's regular seat in the last row.

"Wait." Samar walked in. "Stay."

Like a good little puppy, Aditi stayed. Samar slid his fingers through Misha's and tugged her to the back row to their regular seats. Well, well, well. The witch had won. I wanted to stand up and applaud. Although, I wasn't sure whatever she'd won was worth it.

Mrs Fernandez strode in a second later and I slipped my hand into my pocket to put my phone on silent. Instead, I found the note I'd shoved in there the day before and forgotten about it. Yay for not putting my clothes for wash regularly.

Now that I'd remembered it, my curiosity was like a rabid beast. I couldn't get myself to calm down and concentrate on class. I raised my hand and asked to be excused. Mrs Fernandez grunted her agreement and I scooted from the classroom.

I ran to the bathroom at the end of the corridor and locked myself into a stall. Finally, with trembling fingers, I opened the note.

*I'm sorry.*

That's it? I flipped it over and checked both sides carefully. Nothing. That's all it said.

I'm sorry? Who was sorry? And why?

I shrugged. I may as well get back to class. The mystery note hadn't been as exciting as I'd expected. Fernandez wouldn't be okay with an extended bathroom break and I didn't fancy being on the receiving end of one of her twisted punishments.

I tossed the note into the trash can and headed back to class. I was just in time to solve complex quadratic equations. Joy!

"Katyayani." Fernandez's voice jolted me out of my torturous math work. "What is the answer for problem four?"

"I'm still working on problem two, Ma'am." I flushed at her irritated glower.

"At this speed you can expect to clear your tenth boards next year." She moved past me to bark at someone in the latter rows. I continued to plod through problem two and ended up with a negative answer. That couldn't be right, could it? Fernandez was going to destroy me.

A bony elbow nudged me in the side. I turned my head to see Ashar push his notebook closer to my side. He kept his gaze down so no one would notice.

I glanced down to see his book open to the solution of problem two. His pen tapped idly near the second step. I looked closer. I'd made a mistake with the multiplication of the signs at that step. That's how I'd ended up with a negative answer.

I corrected it quickly in my notebook before Fernandez made her sarcastic, laborious way back to the front. Before she could attack me about problem four again, the bell rang; saving me from further humiliation.

I waited for the general noise level to rise once Fernandez left the room before turning to Ashar.

"Thank you." He looked down his nose at me, which was quite a feat since he was sitting down. "For?"

"For helping me with the math problem." I pulled out my English reader as the teacher walked in.

"I don't know what you're talking about," he said, staring straight ahead.

I would have believed him if it wasn't for the small smile on his lips.

***

I told Bhavya about the note at lunch.

"*I'm sorry.* That's all it said?"

She munched on a cucumber and tomato sandwich that looked far more appetizing than the dal and rice Aunty Sush had packed for me. Could I convince Appa to sign me up for the school lunch plan? I don't think I could survive Aunty Sush's cooking for long. Or I could convince Appa to take over more of the lunch box packing.

"Yep." I spooned one small mouthful of my dal-rice in only to gag at the extra tadka in my mouth.

"Who do you think it could be?" she asked.

I shrugged. The list of people in this school who owed me an apology was as long as Hanumanji's tail.

A couple of kids from Bhavya's class joined us and our table was soon full of laughter and gossip. I let the sheer normalcy of the moment warm my heart. It felt so good. It took me back to my days in Coimbatore. To the days when I'd been truly happy.

"Do you think I could request for a transfer to your section?" I asked Bhavya.

She shook her head. "They don't allow transfers. Some nonsense about learning to make friends wherever you are."

"No one could make friends with the Vipers."

I was aghast at the very thought of trying to be friends with Misha and her gang.

We'd dubbed them the Vipers for how poisonous they were. They'd give the serpent in the Garden of Eden a run for its money.

Bhavya then quickly added, "Ahh but let me tell you; everyone is redeemable."

"Even Satan?"

"The Vipers are Satan's minions." She grinned. "Actually, I think they would give even Satan a run for his money."

"Hey Katya." Aruna, one of the girls at our table leaned forward. "I heard you made it to the relay team. Congratulations."

"Thanks." I smiled. "I love track events."

"If you like basketball too, the school team has tryouts later today."

"I do." Sports had always been my thing. Academics not so much. So this was right up my alley. "I'll be there."

"Ash." The loud shout had my head shooting up. Ashar was walking past our table with his friend.

"Yeah?" He stopped right behind my chair.

"Coming to basketball tryouts today?" Aruna asked.

"Of course."

Of course? Why of course? I bit my tongue to keep from asking.

"Katya is trying out. Do you think she will manage to make it to the mixed team?" Silence. And then…

"I wouldn't know until I see her play."

The gruff response had me prickling with anger. Who did he think he was?

"I didn't know you were the coach of the basketball team to judge me or my performance." I gulped in some more awful dal and rice.

"Not the coach, just the captain."

He had that annoying, small smile on his lips again. Stupid lips. Stupid kissable lips.

I spat out my dal rice. Kissable lips? What was wrong with me? Bhavya looked alarmed. "Are you going to throw up like Misha? I'd like to get out of the way if you are."

"Very funny," I said, as the rest of our table erupted in laughter. I was weirdly aware of Ashar walking away from the table but I didn't turn around.

Across the room Misha and Samar held fort at their crowded table. Mallika was banished to one corner, poor thing. But then, when did betrayal pay off in the long run? It was hard to feel sorry for her after what she'd tried to pull.

"So," Bhavya said.

"So?" I was still watching Samar whisper something into Misha's ear.

"Ashar and you."

"What?" My head snapped back to her.

"What's going on?"

"What?" I squeaked again.

I cleared my throat and tried again. "What are you talking about?"

"I saw the way he looked at you." She grinned.

The way he looked at me? What did she mean 'the way he looked at me'? How had he looked at me? Could I ask? How uncool would I be if I asked?

Nobody had ever considered me cool, so I asked, "How does he look at me?"

Before she could answer, the bell rang and everyone stood up to get back to class. I stared at my dabba of food that was still full and shut it with a sigh. I would have to feed Tommy, the stray dog, near our house again before I got home or I would get grief over bringing home an almost full lunch box.

Tommy was starting to look forward to my return every day. He knew he could rely on me for food and conversation.

I wonder if Tommy would know how Ashar looks at me…

# Fourteen

## Misha

"Hi Misha." Uncle Kannan hovered uncomfortably by my bedroom door.

"Hello," I said warily.

What was this about? We generally existed in a state of armed peace. He didn't mess with me and I didn't mess with him. Katya and I had an unspoken agreement to keep our respective parents out of our feud.

"Sush and I were thinking that maybe all of us could watch a movie together tonight? Order a pizza and some ice cream? Or I could rustle up some deliciously cheesy white pasta?"

Oh dear. The parentals were trying hard for some quality family time. I'd rather they dipped me in honey and let wild ants crawl all over me.

But as I looked into his hopeful face, I realized I couldn't say no. Uncle Kannan was, for lack of a better word, nice. Boring but nice. And I couldn't bring myself to disappoint him.

It would have been easier to say no to my mother if she'd been the one to ask. Of late, she'd done nothing but disappoint me. Returning the favour would have been a piece of cake. That's probably the reason she had sent her husband to represent them.

"Sure." I nodded. "I'll be down in ten minutes."

"Excellent." He disappeared like a genie before I could change my mind. I'm sure he was rushing down the stairs to tell my mother the good news. Family movie night. Ughh.

I loosened my hair and fluffed it up until it fell in loose waves. Took a selfie and posted it on social media.

*Stuck doing fam stuff tonight. Pray for me guys!*

I went down to see Katya sitting on the couch, looking as uncomfortable as I felt. The parentals were arguing over which movie we would watch. As long as they didn't pick a movie with a motivational message for us, I was fine.

I sat down on the couch as far away as possible from Katya. It seemed as though we both did not want to be anywhere near each other. She folded her arms so we didn't touch; even accidentally.

I rolled my eyes and checked my social media profile. 150 likes already with over 40 comments. Good! The 'Pukey' damage had been reversed. Samar's lockdown on liking me had been lifted. My followers were restored and with it the memory of my Puke Gate scandal was diminished. Yay me. But why wasn't I happy? I should be feeling victorious. Instead, I only felt lost and empty within.

A moment later, the movie started. 'Blended'. Oh good, now I felt horrified.

A strangled sound emerged from the other end of the couch. I looked over to see Katya holding a cushion over her face to hold in her laughter.

I laughed. The whole situation was so ridiculous. It was either that or cry. How clueless could the adults be?

And once I started laughing, I couldn't stop.

"It is a funny movie, isn't it?" Uncle Kannan beamed.

Across me, Katya burst into more strangled laughter. She sounded like a frog on its deathbed. This made me laugh even harder.

I could barely see the television screen as tears streamed down my face. The confused parentals couldn't help but shift their glance between Katya and me and then the television screen.

Deciding that it didn't matter what we were laughing at, they settled down with huge bowls of popcorn for all of us.

They'd dimmed the lights, put the air conditioner on and set up enough snacks to feed the entire city. Strangely enough, it was both soothing and enjoyable. I leaned my head back on the couch and watched Drew Barrymore and Adam Sandler fall in love in a typical chaotic, messy, rom-com fashion.

When my mother put her hand on my leg and squeezed, for the first time in ages I didn't feel the urge to shove it off. Instead, I let it rest there as something rather radical dawned on me. Maybe family movie night wasn't so bad after all. Even if it was with some strange, abnormal family add-ons. Ignore that fact and let's face it; this was actually a decent way to spend the evening.

Something that felt an awful lot like peace filled the empty holes inside me as I let my mother draw me in closer.

"The next time we get to choose the movie," I told her. She smiled and planted a kiss on my hair. I'd take that to be a yes.

***

I was finishing up an assignment in French later that evening when Malu called. I'd been waiting for her to make contact.

"Hi Misha." She sounded diffident.

Too late freak, I thought viciously. You should have thought twice before you decided to steal my boyfriend.

"Hi." My cold tone conveyed how I felt crystal clear. Peace and friendship were the last things on my mind.

"I was wondering if you have the guidelines for the Physics assignment. I seem to have lost my sheet."

"I do." I let the words hang in the silence between the two of us.

I could feel her hesitancy in the awkward silence but eventually she asked, "Could you send me a picture in a message?"

"No." I replied unapologetically.

"Misha, please." She pleaded, sounding like she would cry any minute. Who in the world knew Physics was so important to her... Didn't she aspire to be a fashion designer?

"Sorry. I'm busy." I hung up without waiting for her response. It was only after I'd put the phone down that I noticed my other hand. I had it clenched so tight that my pencil had snapped into half.

Damn. Another thing I could blame Malu for. Ex-BFF's are the worst.

The next minute the door opened after a quick knock. Ma stepped in and shut the door behind her.

"Still awake?" she asked, as she sat on the bed.

"Obviously." The anger and hurt from Malu's call had destroyed any happy feelings I'd had earlier that evening. "What do you want, Ma?"

She stiffened, pain tightening her features. "Are we back to this then? I thought we'd taken a step forward this evening."

"Why? Because you showed me some stupid movie?"

I regretted the words as soon as they were out but I wouldn't take them back. The anger and pain inside me wouldn't let me. I needed to hurt her as much as she'd hurt me.

She sighed. A tired sound that made tears prickle my eyes.

"I came to tell you that we'll be coming to school tomorrow. It's career counselling day. They want to talk to us about the electives you'll be choosing and your future plans."

"Okay."

"You're decided then? On doing science?"

"Yes."

"You know," she started, hesitantly. "There are a lot of career options nowadays. It doesn't have to be either Medicine or Engineering anymore. You could even look at…"

"Law?" I interrupted. "Like you? No thanks. I don't want to be a professional liar."

She looked at me in silence. She looked devastated. Good, I thought. Now she knows how I feel.

"Goodnight Misha," she said, finally, getting up to go to the door. "I hope you sleep well."

I would sleep well. I always slept well. I'm not the one with a guilty conscience. I hadn't done anything wrong.

And yet, when it was time to sleep that night, it wasn't in any way peaceful.

# Fifteen

## Katya

"So, Katya." The career counsellor stared down the top of her glasses at me. "You are sure you want to drop Science and opt for Humanities?" I nodded. Beside me, my father shifted restlessly in his seat.

"Do you even realise this will cut off a lot of options for you?"

I nodded again. "Kitty, you're sure?" Appa pitched in, concerned about my future.

"Yes. I know what I want to do later and it doesn't have anything to do with science."

I couldn't wait to be done with all my science and math subjects. Although I needed to pass them in the 10th boards first. And then I will drop them like a hot potato and run as fast as I can in the other direction.

"And what is that?" The counsellor asked, pulling me back from my daydream of tearing up my math and science textbooks and setting them on fire. What a bonfire that would make!

"What?" I asked, having missed her question. I knew she'd asked me something but I wasn't sure what it was.

"What do you want to do? Career wise," Appa clarified, his hand tapping nervously on the table.

"I want to be a psychologist."

The counsellor frowned. "Why not a psychiatrist then? You could still do medicine and then..."

"No." Panic swam through my veins. I could not do more science. Please God. I would never make it through more science.

"I think, Miss, she is happy with taking humanities as an elective and doing Psychology." Appa intervened.

"Okay." It was clear the counsellor didn't think much of my choice. I couldn't care less. I just wanted to be able to go to school without the pit of anxiety in my stomach that opened up every time I thought of the classes I had to get through.

Another few minutes of pointless chit chat between my father and the counsellor and we were done.

While Appa and I were heading out I saw Ashar walk in with his father. I gulped. His father looked terrifying and Ashar looked miserable. He didn't acknowledge me as they walked past, although his father nodded at mine.

I wondered what the story behind that whole scene was. Before I could wonder anymore, Misha and Aunty Sush walked up to us. They both looked red faced and furious. I found myself, unconsciously, slowing my steps. I wanted no part of this family drama.

Appa slowed down too and I had the strangest feeling he wouldn't mind running in the opposite direction. Maybe we could run together.

"All done?" he asked instead, jovially. A little too loudly and jovially. Several other parent and kid combinations turned to look at us, startled.

Aunty Sush nodded, tightlipped. Misha looked bored.

"She wants to be an Engineer just like her father," Aunty Sush gritted out. An Engineer? How exactly was Misha going to manage that with her current grades in science? They were average at best. Certainly nowhere close to the high scores expected of a potential engineering graduate.

"Just like my father." Misha beamed at us.

Counsellor
office

Ahh ok. This was only about hurting her mother. That made more sense than Misha writing the IIT entrance exams.

"Shall we leave?" Aunty Sush asked Appa, a defeated smile etched onto her face.

He nodded and gave me one last hug while Aunty Sush patted me awkwardly on my head. Appa tried to hug Misha too but she turned away at the last moment so he ended up swiping one arm in the air. It escaped nobody's notice that Aunty Sush didn't even look at Misha before they left.

I really needed that psychology degree. How else would I ever understand any of these people?

***

Ashar slid into his seat next to me, still looking mopey and broody. He pulled out his English notebook and opened it to a fresh page. I realized I was staring at his desk like I was hypnotized and turned towards my own book.

English was one of the more peaceful classes. We had an overenthusiastic, chirpy teacher who thought she was motivating us into learning better. She didn't realise she was relaxing us into coasting through the subject. Nothing motivated teenagers quite like fear.

Ooooh. Good one. I scribbled the last line down in my notebook before I forgot it. It would go into my 'Psych Kitty' notebook. I'd taken to writing down my random thoughts and observations in the last year. Along with journaling, it helped me process the insanity that was so much a part of my life.

"Nothing motivated teenagers like fear?" Ashar snorted. "What nonsense is that?"

"It's not nonsense." I defended myself. "It's true." And profound. I kept that last thought to myself.

"And stop looking at my notebook," I added.

"You were looking into mine just a while ago." He shot back.

"Of all the juvenile, idiotic..." My words trailed off as I saw his notebook. It had flipped open to a page filled with notes on Hamlet, the non-detailed text we were assigned for the tenth board exams.

"What?" he asked, his puzzled gaze going from my stunned face to his notebook.

"You wrote that note," I whispered. It was impossible to miss the similarity in handwriting. The 's' had a little swirl to the tail that had struck me even when I'd seen the anonymous 'I'm sorry' note.

He flushed. A wonderful, deep, brick red. I grinned like a maniac. Oh what joy! This moment was everything wonderful. I couldn't suppress my glee.

"What were you sorry about?" I asked.

Unfortunately, I had no hope of getting an answer because Mrs Shetty bustled into the room with enough cheer and goodwill to make a mockery of the tragedy that Hamlet was meant to be. "So, everybody," she beamed, her round face lit up like a Christmas tree. Was she on drugs or something, I wondered. How was it even possible for anyone to be this happy all the time? "How was career counselling?" She bustled around her desk setting up papers and ominous looking files. No one answered. It didn't deter Mrs Shetty one bit.

"Come on, come on. Tell me what all you smart kids want to be when you grow up."

"Misha, are you feeling nauseous?" Someone called from the back.

A few suppressed giggles ran through the room at the heckler's snide remark. Even Mrs Shetty's smile dimmed a little.

"I want to be a psychologist," I said, loudly, into the sudden silence that descended.

Mrs Shetty's head swung towards me, her smile restored.

"How lovely," she said. "And Ashar? What about you?"

I sensed more than just the death glare that Ashar shot at me for drawing unwarranted attention in our direction.

"Doctor," he mumbled, his enthusiasm at par with someone who'd decided to be a grave digger.

"What kind of doctor? Or have you not decided on that as yet?"

Okay, I'd felt bad for her for a minute but now the relentless sweetness was making my teeth ache. "Cardiologist," Ashar growled, startling me to the point that I dropped my pen.

Even Mrs Shetty looked a little taken aback. She decided to drop the interrogation and get back to Hamlet's eternal issues.

I tore off a small piece of paper from the back of my English notebook while the rest of the class rustled through their textbooks for the right page.

*I'm sorry.* I slipped it across to Ashar's desk when no one was looking and then bent my head, industriously, over my own book.

A minute later, a note appeared in my line of vision.

*You should be!* I tapped my pen against my book, contemplating my next move.

*I know what I'm sorry for … what are you sorry for?*

We were no longer passing notes. We were scribbling in my notebook and shoving it at each other.

*Making the mistake of sending you a note in the first place!*

I was still grinning to myself when Mrs Shetty asked, "Is Hamlet funny, Katyayani?"

"Umm, no?"

"Are you asking me or telling me?" This was the first time I'd seen her look angry. Her flinty eyes bored into me. So much for feeling sorry for her earlier.

I opened my mouth to answer but nothing came out. Embarrassment coursed through me as I felt the collective weight of the class's gaze fall upon me.

Before my eyes, Mrs Shetty seemed to deflate suddenly. All the anger left her and she looked sad and defeated. I was back to feeling sorry for her.

I was going to apologise for not paying attention but she turned her back on me and went to write something on the blackboard. My notebook was pushed back in front of me with a new note with Ashar's scribbly handwriting on it.

*Nothing motivated teenagers quite like fear!*

I snorted. Helpless laughter bubbled up inside me until I caught sight of what Mrs Shetty was writing on the board.

**A 1000 word assignment on Hamlet as a revenge tragedy – due tomorrow!**

Oh dear. My already non-existent popularity in this class tanked even further. Truly, nothing motivated teenagers quite like fear! I feared I may not make it to class tomorrow.

# Sixteen

## Misha

"What's for dinner?" My mother didn't bother to look at me as she continued to type away furiously on her laptop.

"Ma?" I raised my voice. "Dinner?"

"Go look in the fridge." She waved a hand over her shoulder. "There will be something there."

Oh. Attitude alert!

I opened the fridge and stuck my head in. Salty rajma, undercooked rice, plain salad, burnt aloo. Everything looked revoltingly unappetizing.

"Can I order something?" I asked. "I don't feel like eating any of this."

She shrugged, continuing to ignore me.

Fine by me. I was happier when I was ignored. A slight twinge inside me told me I was lying to myself but it didn't matter. I'd just ignore it like everyone ignored me.

I ordered a chicken and broccoli pasta with white sauce, using my mother's card to pay. She silently held out her phone to me. I swiped it open and retrieved the OTP I needed.

I was about to hand over the phone back to her when a message notification flashed across the screen.

From Arunoday, my father. I quickly tapped the message open and scrolled through their last chat.

*We need to talk about Misha.*

*I'm busy. I told you, I'm on tour for the rest of the month.*

*Arun, she's out of control. I don't know how to handle it anymore. Surely, you have some time to speak to her.*

*Not right now, Sush. You wanted custody of her. You deal with it.*

*Maybe you could take her for a few months? A change of scene…*

And then, the message that just popped up.

*Sorry, no. I can't.*

I shoved the phone back at her and left the room. She didn't look up from her laptop.

I was halfway up the stairs when I saw them. Katya and her father. I stared.

Uncle Kannan was wearing a suit that didn't fit very well and Katya was wearing slim fit jeans with a one shoulder, pale pink top that made her look like a strawberry cupcake. She had left her hair loose and swept it up on one side with a clip. She even had makeup on. Until now, I didn't even know she owned makeup of any kind. I hoped she hadn't dipped into my stash!

They were laughing at some inside joke that made my own insides churn. I hated them. I hated everyone.

"Misha!" Uncle Kannan spotted me. "How was school today?"

I didn't answer. It was obviously a polite attempt to make conversation when they clearly were due to be elsewhere and I didn't see the point of humouring it.

"Going out?" I asked, even as my phone pinged with my dinner update. Pasta for one. Yay me!

"Yes, Katya and I have a date tonight," he said, proudly. "I'm going to be her first date."

Katya smiled up at him, her normally pointy face soft and sweet.

Jealousy, resentment, loneliness and something else that I couldn't identify, welled up inside me.

"If you think you're her first date, you're delusional," I said, my words slicing through their happy haze. I looked at Katya, who looked stricken. "And you're a liar, Kitty."

I spat the nickname out at them. I'd overheard the parentals discussing the whole nonsense about my mother calling her by the nickname her late mother had given her and how upset she'd gotten. I'd thought it was silly and dramatic then but now, all it came down to, was a weapon. And one that did its job well from the look on Katya's face.

***

I threw myself on the bed, angry tears burning my eyes. Stupid people. Stupid date. Stupid smiles. Stupid everything.

My door slammed open.

"What the hell is wrong with you?" My mother looked like she was going to start spewing flames.

"Did your darling husband come running to you to complain?" I asked, snidely.

"Is that the only thing bothering you? That I've heard about it? Your bad behaviour, on its own, doesn't make a difference to you?"

My bad behaviour. I wanted to laugh. The only thing everyone could see was my bad behaviour. What about theirs?

My parents got divorced so my mother could marry the man she'd fallen in love with.

My father called me once a month to ask if I needed anything. He never asked me anything beyond that.

My mother was now trying to get rid of me. My father didn't want me. So where do I go now? To an orphanage?

"I asked you a question." My mother's voice rose.

"You asked me several questions. Which one should I answer first?"

To my surprise, my mother collapsed on to the bed beside me.

"I can't do this anymore, Misha." She buried her face in her hands. "Tell me what I need to do to make things work. Please just tell me."

I didn't answer. How could she make it work? She was the one who had destroyed everything. Pa and she hadn't been happy. I knew that. It was impossible to miss. The fights, the screaming, the long silences.

But at least they had been together. We had been a family. We had lived in one house. And I could see my father. I still *had* a father. And then she had an affair with Uncle Kannan. And here we were.

"Please?" she whispered again. I turned my face away from her and looked out of the window. There was a crow sitting on the tree branch outside which stared back at me. I wonder what it made of all the drama that went on in our house.

My phone vibrated with a message from Samar.

*Want to tandem watch a movie?*

No. I didn't want to tandem watch a movie. I didn't want to tandem do anything with the asshole who'd betrayed and humiliated me so publicly. I hadn't forgotten anything he'd done. Rage burned in my chest again. I wanted to scream, to shout, to break something.

Instead, I replied, '*Yes. Give me a few.*'

"Go away, Ma," I said to my silent mother. "That's how you can fix this. By just staying away."

She left silently, without another word. The click of the door sounded like a gunshot inside my head.

I video called Samar. He answered on the first ring. His hair flopped into his eyes and he lounged on his bed, shirtless.

I rolled my eyes at him. "You don't need to try so hard, Sam."

"I don't need to try at all," he smirked.

I ignored the smug expression on his face and asked, "What movie do you want to watch?"

"Actually." Samar grabbed a pillow and rolled on to his stomach. "I want to watch something different."

"Really?" I was surprised. Samar didn't really go for different. He always wanted to watch action, fantasy and superheroes, not necessarily in that order.

"Yeah." He smiled at me. I smiled back, uneasily. I didn't like the sound of this.

"Don't tell me you want to watch some adult movie or something?"

"Porn? Na." He shook his head, glossy, silky hair flying from side to side like he was featuring in some shampoo advertisement. I sighed in relief. As long as it wasn't that, I was fine. Anything else I could handle.

"I want to watch you," he said, his smile widening.

"Me?" I laughed, ridiculously touched. Samar wasn't usually romantic and rarely said sweet things like this. "You are watching me, silly."

"Don't act dumb." His smile disappeared for a moment before appearing again. "I want to watch *you*."

My mouth went dry. He couldn't mean… could he?

"What do you mean?" I asked, praying to all the Gods that I was wrong about what I thought he meant.

"I want to watch you naked, Mish," he purred. "Come on. Take your clothes off."

# Seventeen

## Katya

"Who the hell does she think she is?" I raged, stomping up and down the sidewalk outside our home as my silent father stood by awkwardly.

Misha had definitely ruined our date night. She'd ruined my birthday week. Appa had already said we couldn't exclude the mother-daughter duo from my actual birthday so we'd planned this earlier in the week. And now, it was ruined. Everything was ruined. Just like it had been from the day Misha Banerjee had entered my life.

"I hate her!!" The words came out as a scream.

Appa flinched. "Don't say that, Kitty."

"Don't say that?" I was shrieking now. People were starting to stare. "What am I allowed to say? Am I even allowed to say ANYTHING?"

My father didn't respond. He looked more defeated than ever. When he finally spoke it was to say, "Our reservations are for eight o' clock. They won't hold the table for long. Are we going or no?"

I stared at him. "What happened to you, Appa?" The words were a bare whisper. "You were never like this. Amma would have…"

"Amma is dead." He hadn't raised his voice but the words hit me like I'd been punched hard in my stomach. "She is dead, Katyayani, and she is not coming back. What Amma would have or wouldn't have done is not relevant anymore. The only thing that matters is what we do now. You. Me. Sush. Misha."

He raked his hands through his thick salt and pepper hair. "Do you think by not accepting our situation, Misha and you are going to accomplish anything other than being miserable?"

"Our situation?" For the first time in my life, I felt violent. I wanted to hit him. I wanted to hurt him. "OUR situation is your fault. Yours and Aunty Sush's." I spat the words at him.

"Stop it, Katya. This is not the place or time for this conversation."

"Then when is it? When is it the place or the time? Was it when you told me you were marrying Aunty Sush? Was it when you decided we were moving to Bangalore? Was it when you changed my school, my friends, my entire life without even asking me if that was what I wanted? When was it the place or the time, Appa? When??"

People were actually stopping to stare at us now. Appa noticed too. "Let's go home now." He took my arm and tried to tug me towards the apartment. "We can talk at home."

"That's not home." My voice rose to a hysterical shriek. I felt like I was standing outside of myself and watching this complete mess. I desperately wanted to tell myself to stop but I couldn't. All I could do was watch in horror. "That's not my home."

Tears welled up inside me and spilled over. An endless fountain of them. "I want to go home!" I wailed. "I want to go to my home. I want my Amma back. I want my home back. I want my life back." The words trailed off into a whisper.

"Kitty," Appa whispered, appalled. He came forward to pull me into a hug but I moved away. I didn't want him touching me right now. I didn't want anyone touching me right now.

My body shook with the force of my sobs. I sat down on the dusty pavement and cried until it felt like there was nothing left inside me. No pain, no hurt, no grief. Nothing.

When my sobs eventually dwindled, I felt my father put an arm around me and guide me up the small lane and back into the house. This time I let him.

***

"Are you okay?"

I looked up from my spot in the corner of the kindergarten playground to see Ashar looking down at me.

"Sure." I shrugged. "Why wouldn't I be?"

He sat down beside me on the tiny, cement bench. We looked at the little kids running around the swings and the jungle gym. A small scuffle was breaking out near the slide and an attendant rushed to sort it out.

"Why are you here and not in the cafeteria?" he asked, when the victor of the scuffle was carted away to meet the teacher.

"How did you find me?"

"I planted a GPS tracker in your backpack. I know where you are at all times."

I turned to look at him. "It's a good thing you're going to be a cardiologist. I'm fairly certain a career in comedy is out of the question." His smile disappeared. He looked out at the crowded playground.

"I saw you turn away from the cafeteria and come here. So, I followed you."

"A creepy, stalker type follow?"

"A friend who is worried about you follow."

The tips of his ears turned bright red. Interesting…

"So, we are friends now? A few days back you were screaming that you weren't my friend."

"I apologised for that," he said, gruffly.

He had. I stayed quiet, a little ashamed of my own behaviour.

"I'm sorry," I said now. "I'm not having the best day."

"That's obvious from your red eyes and even redder nose."

Oh Mr Red Ears was going to make fun of me, was he? I was about to launch into a blistering retort when…

"Why are you sad, Katya?"

Why was I sad? No one had asked me that question till now. My eyes welled up with tears again. Stupid, weak, senseless, pointless tears.

I blinked them back and kept my gaze on the little kids now digging in the sand pit.

"Did you always want to be a cardiologist?" I asked in a bid to change the topic.

"I don't even want to be one now."

"But," I turned my head to look at him. His profile looked angry, bitter and … sad. "Didn't you say that was what you were going to be?"

"That is what I'm going to be. Doesn't mean it's what I want to be." Definitely sad.

"What do you want to be?" He was quiet for so long that I thought he wasn't going to answer.

"I want to be a political journalist."

"And you aren't doing that because?"

He rested his head on his folded arms and turned his face to look at me, mimicking my pose.

"Because my father is a cardiologist and nothing else is acceptable. Especially not a degree in English Literature."

I didn't know what to say to that so I decided not to say anything at all.

"Why do you want to be a psychologist?"

"So I can figure myself and my life out," I said, promptly.

He laughed. "So you want to be your own first patient?"

"Yep. Once I've sorted myself out, I'll worry about the patients who might have the misfortune to wander into my clinic."

Ashar smiled; a sweet, sweet smile that stirred some strange feelings inside me. All sorts of feelings. Very complicated feelings. My heart started to thud faster. Maybe I needed a cardiologist? I laughed at my own sad joke.

"What's so funny?" he asked.

I shook my head. "Thank you for stalking me."

He shrugged, his ears turning red again. "We should get back to class. Lunch break is almost over."

I sighed. We had Chemistry now so I had another forty-five minutes of struggling to understand whatever came out of the teacher's mouth.

Ashar held out his hand to pull me up, a small smile tugging at his lips. "Don't be sad, Katya. I'll let you copy from my notes again."

And just like that Chemistry got a lot more interesting.

# Eighteen

## Misha

I was in disgrace. For the way I'd behaved with Katya and her father, I was banished to my room which to be honest wasn't any kind of punishment. I felt like I was being rewarded. It wasn't like I wanted to speak to any of those losers.

I plonked down on the bed and stared at the ceiling. Today was a wonderful day. I got to spend it on my own, mulling all the ways in which I could make life interesting for myself and others in it. Of course, my interesting was not always the same as their interesting.

My phone rang. Samar. I glanced at it and ignored his call. I didn't want to talk right now. He'd made me uncomfortable last night and I wasn't ready to feel that way again.

A message popped up on my screen. I swiped it open.

*Call me babe.*

I ignored it and went back to contemplating the ceiling. I really did enjoy being banished.

A knock on my door surprised me. This was turning out to be a short banishment, to my eternal disappointment. Uncle Kannan stepped in and surprise turned to shock. The two of us have skirted around each other like wary participants in a reality show. This would probably be our first conversation without either of the other two participants stuck in this house of horrors with us.

"Hello." He smiled, uneasily. "May I come in?"

"You're already in." I pointed out. What was his endgame? What did he want?

He looked even more uncomfortable at that.

"I can leave if you want me to..." His voice trailed off.

I shrugged, unsure of how to respond to that. I didn't necessarily want to have a conversation with him but I couldn't say that. Even I had some lines I didn't want to cross.

"I was wondering..." He seemed to struggle to find the right words. "I was wondering," he tried again. "If you would like to spend some time with me?"

My mouth fell open in shock. "With you?"

He shifted his body weight from one foot to the other, hitched his pants up. It never ceased to amaze me that this was the man my mother had left my father for. My father was handsome, sophisticated, successful... Uncle Kannan was ... well, he was awkward. I didn't get it. I truly didn't.

He was still standing there waiting for me to answer. So I said the only thing that popped into my head.

"Why?"

"Why?" he repeated.

"Why do you want to spend time with me?" I was genuinely baffled. Katya and he were such a team; I didn't really think he had any need for another daughter-type person in his life.

"I want to spend time with you," he said, as he sat on my bed, "because we all live together in this house. We also are a part of this mashed up family. And mostly because Sush loves you and I would like us to form some kind of equation."

I didn't respond.

"I am not trying to be your father. I know you already have one. I also know that you love him very much. I am just trying to have a relationship with you. What that relationship would be … that's up to the two of us, I think? To figure out? Maybe friends? Maybe an uncle type? But something at least?"

"Something more than housemates?" I quipped. I couldn't be a witch in the face of his earnestness. Also, he was wrong about me loving my father very much. My father and I loved each other the basic amount needed for that relationship to exist.

He smiled, some of his unease melting away. "Something more than that, yes."

I went to sit beside him on the bed. "And what about Katya?"

"Kitty?" His forehead creased in confusion. "What about her?"

"I don't think she will like you having any kind of equation with me, Uncle Kannan."

"I have space in my life for more than one relationship, Misha. Space in my heart too. Why don't you leave Kitty to me?"

Maybe now I could see what my mother saw in him. He was nice. Too freaking nice for me to be snide. In fact, too nice for me to shut down like I normally would.

"Okay," I said, finally. "I'll leave Kitty to you. I'll also leave Sush to you if you don't mind."

He laughed, a startled sound. "She loves you very much you know."

"No, I don't know." I stood up from the bed. Some kind of equation was fine but we were not having heart to hearts. That wasn't part of the deal.

I stepped away from him so he knew that hugs were not part of the deal too. He gave me an awkward pat on my shoulder and with a last kind smile, he left.

Well, well, well … Imagine that! I was actually jealous of Kitty Katyayani Shankar.

***

I answered Samar's call after my new house BFF left my room.

"What's up?" I asked, my mind still on the conversation with Uncle Kannan.

"Did you think about it?" he asked.

"It?" The naked thing? My mind snapped to attention. He was like a dog with a bone. "Not now, Samar."

Not now, not ever.

"My parents are at home," I improvised when he glowered at me through the phone screen. I needed to distract him before this blew up into a situation I couldn't control.

"Want to know something funny?" I asked.

"What?" He was still sulking.

I hesitated, Uncle Kannan's sweet, earnest face flashing before my eyes. I couldn't do this.

"I have to go," Samar interrupted my thoughts. "If you're not going to strip or do anything interesting, I have…"

"Katya's nickname is Kitty," I blurted out, desperation taking over. "It's what her mother used to call her before she died." Something deep inside me quaked. I knew I had certainly crossed a line. I knew that but I didn't know how to go back from here.

Samar stared at me. "What? Like cat? What's the big deal in that?"

"Really, Sam." I forced myself to sound scornful. "Kitty – Pussy? I thought you would make the connection by now."

A slow smile spread across his face. "You're a real freak," he laughed.

"But I'm your freak, honey," I whispered back even as I avoided meeting my own eyes in the mirror that hung on the wall across from me.

"Yes. That you are. My freak. Only mine." Samar blew me a kiss. "Okay listen," he said, now. "If you don't want to take it off now, send me a picture later at least."

And we were back to that. I was not sending him nudes. I may be a freak but I wasn't a stupid one.

"I told you my parents are here." I sat up in bed, a vague unease coursing through me.

"Fine, fine." He scrubbed a hand over his head. "Okay. How about a compromise?A compromise? Samar didn't know the meaning of the word. I waited for him to spell it out.

"Show me your tits at least."

"Samar!" I growled.

"Come on, Misha. Don't be such a prude. It's not like I haven't seen them before."

Of course he had. We'd made out before. We'd kissed and felt each other up but this … on a call. It made me uncomfortable.

"Samar, I don't…"

"Fine. Be a f*%$ing pain in the f*%$ing ass then." He shook his head. "I have to go."

"Samar wait!" The disgust in his voice had my heart racing. What was the harm anyway? Like he said, he'd already seen them. I whipped my shirt off before I could change my mind. I pulled my sports bra off and stared at him, cheeks flushing. It felt like my entire body was on fire.

Samar smiled. His happiness and approval beamed through the stupid phone and right through to me. Strangely, it made me want to weep.

"Okay?" I asked, quickly pulling my shirt back on even before he could respond.

"Okay," he said. "I love you."

I wanted to say it back but the words just wouldn't come. They seemed to be stuck in the same pit in my stomach that my heart had sunk into.

Samar didn't bother waiting for my response. He waved and disconnected before I said another word.

I stared at my blank phone, my face and body still feeling like it was aflame. My phone vibrated. It was a message from Samar.

*Don't tell your 'sister' but I have a surprise planned for her.*

I bolted for the bathroom. My dinner came up, burning a fiery trail of regret and shame through me. Once I got it all out, I splashed my still burning face with cold water. It didn't help. Nothing was going to help now.

# Nineteen

## Katya

The basketball court at St. Thomas was a dry, patchy expanse of ground with chalk outlines marking the extent of the court. I lined up with the rest of the wannabes as we waited for the PHE Coach Mr Sebastian to finish with his pep talk.

He was still explaining to us about how there was a girls team and a boys team and a mixed team. The mixed team comprised of the best players from both the other teams. The captain of both the boys' team and the mixed team was none other than His Highness Mr Ashar, who currently stood beside the coach and grinned at me. The geeky nerds of St. Thomas had secret depths to them.

I pretended to ignore him and took my place as we were divided into teams and the first game started. And then I forgot everything but the thrill of playing a sport. It had always been like this with me. Sports, any kind of physical activity, had the ability to take me away from my life and everything in it.

My team was leading by a basket when the whistle blew for halftime. I came to a panting halt, exhilaration flowing through me. Coach Sebastian beckoned me over. I jogged over to where he stood, His Highness still by his side.

"You're very good, Katyayani," he observed. "Did you play for your previous school?" I nodded, still panting too hard to get a word out.

"Interesting." He eyed me like I was a prize cow available at the market. "I don't think you need to tryout anymore. You've made it to the team."

I had? I grinned, joy streaming through me. I got to play more? This was like the best birthday present ever.

"Both in the girls' team and the mixed team."

My smile dimmed a bit. His Highness was going to be my captain. Aarrgghh.

Ashar grinned at me again. It was fairly obvious he knew what was going through my mind. I ignored him and went to sit down on the bench behind them. The tryouts started again and I watched with half a mind. The other half stayed on the conversation between the coach and Ashar.

They debated, argued and discussed the tryouts like equals. I was surprised. In my previous school, when the coach blew his whistle, we jumped to do his bidding. There were no discussions.

Finally, the tryouts wound down and the shortlisted candidates were given a time later that week for a final tryout.

"Katyayani." Coach beckoned me over. "You're on the team but there is one small problem."

Problem? I stared my gaze shifting from his face to Ashar's blank one. Was I supposed to solve this little riddle or were they going to actually tell me what the problem was?

"You can't be on both the basketball and the track team," Coach said, abruptly. "You won't have the bandwidth of time for the amount of practice required and more importantly, school policy encourages you to pursue and train well in one sport."

I looked from one to the other. "So are you saying I can't be part of the basketball team?"

"No," Coach replied. "I'm saying you have to choose."

"Oh!" My face cleared instantly. "Basketball."

Coach raised an eyebrow. "Don't you want to think about it?"

"No." I shook my head, my braid whipping from side to side. "I choose basketball."

No Misha. No Puke Gate giggles. And then there was … I hated to admit it but basketball had Ashar. Yes, yes … I know. I singlehandedly put the feminist movement back by a few years by choosing something because of a boy. But, come on basketball and him. This choice was easy peasy lemon squeezy.

Ashar grinned at me. "Want to play some one-on-one after school today?"

Oh how I wanted some one-on-one! If only he knew… But, I shrugged and tried to play it cool. "I have math tuitions this evening. Maybe some other time."

"Sure." With one last goodbye to the coach, he sauntered off.

Sure? That's it. What the hell happened to 'guys will be keener if you play it cool?' By the time I figured out the answer to that, he'd disappeared from sight.

Great. I'd been so cool, he'd frozen me out.

***

"Hey Katya," Samar called out from across the field as I walked back towards class to collect my things.

I groaned. What did that creep want? I turned and waited for him to come closer.

Had I once thought he was the best looking guy I'd ever seen? He still looked very good. But only from a distance. When he came closer, you could see the mean eyes, the thin lips and that irritating smirk. What Misha saw in him, I would never understand.

"Where are you going babe?" he asked, as he stopped right in front of me.

“My name is Katya,” I told him, coolly. “And I am not your babe.”

“Are you sure about that?” he smirked, coming closer.

I took a step back. He was invading my personal space and making me uncomfortable.

“What the hell has gotten into you?”

I looked around but the ground was mostly empty. Almost everyone had gone back to the classrooms. In the distance, I saw a couple of helpers dismantle some sports equipment and pack it up.

I backed away from him. “I need to get my things from class.”

“I’ll walk with you,” he said. “I have to pack up as well.”

We walked in silence, our footsteps echoing through the fast emptying corridors. Today was Aunty Sush’s turn to pick us up and she was usually late. But I still hurried to get back to our classroom, which was on the other end of this massive campus. Samar was kind of creeping me out.

As we got closer to our class, my footsteps slowed. There was a crowd gathered near the entrance. A giggling, whispering crowd. “I have a little surprise for you.” Samar leaned in close and whispered in my ear. My feet stopped moving. Everything inside me froze. What had he done?

Samar turned towards me and started to walk backwards. He winked, a charming grin spreading across his face. *If Evil had a face, this was it.*

All around me tenth graders from our section and others were nudging each other and glancing at me. I forced myself to walk forward. The crowd parted for me like I was Moses parting the Red Sea.

I saw the picture stuck on the display board first. It was taken from my social media profile. A picture of my mother and me, taken about a year before she died. She had her arms around my shoulders and was beaming. A smile on her big, bright and happy face.

A voice bubble was stuck on the board. It said, "Have you met my daughter, Pussy? I mean, Kitty!" And then beneath that, "Hey Pussy … here pussy… Are you wet, Pussy?"

I felt like a giant rock was crushing my chest. The voices faded into the background as I stared at the wall. They'd taken the one person I loved more than anything else in the world, taken the most precious memory I'd had of her and they'd … they'd defiled it.

Rage swept through me. A tidal wave of fury that washed away every semblance of control. I launched myself at the wall and started tearing at the words near my mother's mouth. I didn't realise I was screaming just as I didn't know tears were pouring down my face.

I was dimly aware of the fact that silence had descended on the room. A shocked, wary silence.

Two pairs of hands appeared beside me. Bhavya and Ashar. I left the ripping of the vicious words to them and gently peeled the picture in the centre of the board.

I rolled it up and cradled it to my chest, tears dripping on to my shirt and soaking through the front. Bhavya and Ashar had cleared out the rest of the paper from the board and dumped it in the bin.

I stared at the crowd watching us. Samar and Misha stood at the front. He looked wary. My gaze skipped over him. That vicious sleazeball didn't deserve my attention. I locked eyes with Misha. Shame and regret were plastered all over her face.

I held her gaze as I stepped forward. She stepped back. It gave me no pleasure and yet, I walked forward and continued to force her to give ground.

A teacher appeared in the doorway, demanding to know what the ruckus was all about. I didn't bother to look to see who it was. I didn't care.

I strode towards them until Misha stopped backing away. I stopped right in front of them.

"The two of you deserve each other." My words were quiet, even and steady, even as the tears continued to flow.

Misha flinched. She stepped out of my way. I walked past her and the perplexed teacher. I left the room, my mother clutched to my heart. I didn't look back.

# Twenty

## Misha

I scrolled through the posts and reels on social media. Samar, of course, led the pack. Cat videos and pictures, especially drenched, soaking wet ones seemed to be the trending visuals with the St. Thomas set.

I flung the phone down. I couldn't look at the screen anymore. Bile churned in my stomach. Luckily, I hadn't eaten anything yet or it would have come up by now. I hadn't seen Katya since I came home. I hadn't seen her since she walked past me in the classroom holding her mother's picture close to her heart.

Something clenched inside me at the memory. Nausea rose in a sickening wave. I lurched to my feet and ran to the bathroom.

I was just emptying whatever little was there in my stomach when I heard my mother walk in.

"Mishti?" she called. "I mean, Misha," she corrected herself. My stomach did the clenching thing again at the hesitancy in her voice. "Where are you?"

I didn't have the energy to push myself up from the bathroom floor. "Here," I called out, resting my head against the wall behind me.

Her worried face appeared at the door a minute later. "Did you throw up again?" she exclaimed. "What is going on? Is it the heat?"

I chuckled. "Ma, it's winter." When she only stared at me in confusion, I added, "In Bangalore. What heat?"

She didn't smile. I let her pick me up off the floor and help me rinse my face and mouth out before taking me to the bedroom. I dropped down on the bed and buried my face in my pillow.

"I think we should have some tests done," she said, quietly. "This can't be just a case of food poisoning."

I didn't answer. Fatigue swept through me even as my phone vibrated with messages near my head. I didn't have the energy to check or the face with which to see what was happening now.

"Mishti?"

This time when she stroked her hand through my hair, I turned into the touch. Tears gathered in my eyes but I blinked them back.

"It's okay, baby," Ma crooned. "I'll make an appointment with the doctor tomorrow. We'll get this sorted out and you'll be just fine soon."

She kissed me gently on the top of my head and stood. "I'm going to go get you some buttermilk to settle your stomach and then the two of us can watch a movie on your laptop together. Just the two of us, like old times. How does that sound?"

The tears choked my throat until a response was impossible. Ma sighed, the disappointed sound echoing in the silent room.

"I'll just bring the buttermilk up and leave it here then," she said, at last.

I heard the door click shut behind her. I couldn't snuggle with my mother and watch movies. Not after what I'd done. Not after what I'd allowed Samar to do to Katya.

I didn't deserve it. Fatigue, shame and guilt swirled together until I finally fell asleep. Much before my mother managed to make something as simple as buttermilk and deliver it to my room.

I didn't feel her hand stroking through my hair. I didn't feel her lips graze my forehead. I didn't hear her whisper 'I love you'.

I didn't hear anything except for the dark, bitter voices of my pain that haunted my thoughts, my dreams and on some days, my very existence.

***

I ran into Katya on the landing outside our bedroom doors. I expected anger. I expected tears. I expected screams. I didn't expect the flat, blank stare that looked right through me.

"Katya." I stopped her with a hand on her arm. I didn't know what I planned to say but I wanted to say something. Anything.

She paused, looked down to where my fingers touched her. I slowly withdrew it.

"Please don't ever touch me again." The tone was polite. The words anything but.

She walked away, leaving me standing on the landing alone. As alone as it was possible to be with self loathing cradling you in a hug.

I followed in her wake, wondering if she was going to tell the parentals what had happened. I needn't have worried. The four of us sat down to a breakfast of cornflakes and milk in silence. I noticed her father shooting worried glances in Katya's direction but she kept her head down and ate like she was all alone in the room.

Being a Sunday, all four of us were at home. Usually, Samar picked me up and we hung out at his place but today, I wasn't in the mood to be around him.

"Misha." My mother's voice snapped me out of my thoughts. "I've made an appointment with the doctor for eleven this morning."

"I'll drive you," Uncle Kannan offered. Ma nodded, gratefully. Anyone would be grateful not to drive in Bangalore traffic.

"Katya." Uncle Kannan turned to her. "Will you be okay on your own?" She nodded, her eyes on her bowl of cereal. Uncle Kannan's brow creased but he seemed to shelve the question in his mind for now.

"I will get ready and come," he said. He wiped his mouth with a napkin and stood. He shuffled out of the room in his cotton kurta pyjama and kolhapuri chappals. I tried not to notice the kiss he pressed onto Katya's bent head before he left.

"Katya," Ma's bright voice shattered the uneasy silence. "One of my friends mentioned a new bookshop that's opened close by. Would you like to go once we are back from the hospital?"

Wonderful. A sour taste filled my mouth. Katya got trips to bookstores. I got trips to the hospital.

"Thank you but not today," she said, her voice wafer thin and barely audible.

Ma looked disappointed, I thought with vicious pleasure.

"Misha." She turned on me next. "Go get changed. I'm all ready to leave." I scooped the last spoonful from my bowl and pushed back from the table.

"Misha!"

I was almost to the door when Ma's voice stopped me.

“Please put your bowl in the sink.”

I growled and stomped back to the table. I grabbed the bowl with its spoon and dumped it in the sink. Katya didn't look up through the whole commotion. Ma just watched me with tired eyes. I stormed out of the room, irritation and guilt tagging along with me like a big, dark cloud.

I was halfway up the stairs when the doorbell rang. I ran down again and opened it.

Ashar stood on our doorstep, looking uncomfortable and sweaty. How he managed to sweat in this winter chill was a mystery.

“Hi,” he said, lifting one hand in a weird, shifty wave.

I raised an eyebrow and stared at him. “What are you doing here?”

He squared his shoulders and stared me down. “I'm here to see Katya. Could you please let her know I'm here?”

“Katya and you?” I laughed. “Really?”

He stiffened.

“I didn't mean…” I was trying to explain my reaction. “I was just surprised that's all.” But Ashar wasn't interested in what I had to say.

“I know what you meant. Could you please call her?” He cut through my awkward explanation. “I just want to know if she's okay. She isn't answering any of my calls or texts.”

I stared at him. A jealous serpent coiled inside me, rearing its head. I'd been sick in front of the entire class, been cheated on by my boyfriend, humiliated on social media and trolled viciously and not one person had bothered to ask if I was okay. Not One Person.

I raised my voice and yelled, "Hey Kitty. Your boyfriend is here." Ashar blanched. For a second, I thought he'd either faint or turn and run away. Instead, he found the backbone to stand his ground and glare at me.

Uncle Kannan came thundering down the stairs. "What? Who? What did you say?"

Ma and Katya emerged from the dining room. For a moment, we all just stood and stared at each other.

If there was ever a scene for someone to shout 'Action,' this was it. But then, as dramatic as our lives were, we weren't actually a movie script come to life. We were just us.

***

The doctor across the table scribbled on her prescription pad.

"I'd like you to get all these tests done." She handed the paper to Ma who took it and scanned it. "Based on the results, we can see which course of action we should take."

Ma nodded. "Is there anything to worry?" she asked.

"We won't know until we get the test results. Also," she hesitated, glancing over at me. "I would suggest a meeting with a counsellor. While I can't say for sure until I see the results, I suspect we might be dealing with an eating disorder."

She watched me carefully for my reaction. I stared back at her, the same bland expression on my face. An eating disorder? Sure, why not? It would certainly be the icing on the fucked up cake that was my life.

"A counsellor?" Ma sounded panicked. "You're saying this could be a mental issue?" I snickered. "What's so funny?" Ma glared at me. "Do you realise how serious this is?"

"The fact that you are surprised that this might be a mental issue is funny." I laughed. "Remember me? Your mental daughter? The one you screwed up?"

"Stop it," she cried. "It's not funny."

The genuine tears sparkling in her eyes stopped me from continuing with any more of my not so funny jokes.

"Could you recommend a good counsellor?" she asked the doctor who nodded. I didn't make eye contact with either of them. The fatigue was back, dragging me down. Maybe I really did need help.

The silence in the car was deafening on the way back. Uncle Kannan had opted to stay home after my 'Katya's boyfriend bombshell' so Ma was driving with a single minded focus that had very little to do with the traffic and a lot to do with her bothersome daughter.

I stared out of the window. Was this all there was to my life? Sullen silences, aggressive confrontations, backstabbing strategies? The now familiar fatigue floated through me like a misty cloud soaking into my bones.

I leaned my head back and closed my eyes, letting it take over.

"This can't go on forever, Misha," my mother said.

The words seemed to reach me from far, far away. I snuggled into the dark cloud of fatigue and tried to block her out.

"I'm scheduling the appointment with the counsellor as soon as possible." Her hands clenched around the steering wheel. "And then we'll see."

I suppose we would. But I didn't think my mother would like what she'd see. I certainly didn't.

She sighed. "Can't you talk to me? Like we used to talk?"

I kept my eyes shut and my mouth shut tighter.

"I miss you, Mishti." Her voice broke on the last word. "I miss my sweet baby girl."

My eyes snapped open. "Why?" I demanded, my voice a rough croak. "Why do you miss me? Don't you have Katya to take my place? She is the perfect, well-behaved daughter after all."

"Is that what you think?" Ma pulled up at a traffic light that was red and turned to face me. "That I replaced you with Katya."

"And Pa with Uncle Kannan," I spat at her. "Why did you drag me along to your new readymade family? Was it because I was too old to be dropped off at an orphanage?"

A cacophony of horns blaring started from behind us. The light had turned green. My mother turned back to face forward and put the car in gear.

We drove home in silence. A painful silence that echoed with my screamed accusations. There was no going back from here.

# Twenty-One

## Katya

Ashar and I sat across each other in uncomfortable silence. My father pottered around in the kitchen making far too much noise for someone who was just supposed to be cooking.

"You weren't answering any of my messages and calls, so I thought I'd check on you to see if you were okay."

I shrugged. I didn't feel like talking. But how long could we sit like this? "How did you know where I lived?" I asked, finally.

"I asked Bhavya," he answered, looking grateful that I'd broken the awkward silence. "She told me."

Bhavya had asked for my address a few weeks earlier when we'd been making plans to visit each other's homes and hang out. Plans that had never materialised.

Ashar was looking at me for a response. I nodded, not sure what to add to that. Ashar leaned forward. "Do you want me to go?" I opened my mouth to say yes. Instead, what came out was, "Do you want to watch a movie?"

"Sure," he said, looking visibly relieved. "Which one?"

"Anything." I shrugged, again. I'd gotten very shruggy lately. "Do you want to watch 'Yes Day'?"

"Sure," he said again, making room next to him for me. He was sitting on the couch facing the television. I sat down next to him making sure I left enough space between us to keep my father from banging some more pots and pans around in the kitchen.

Once the sound from the television was loud enough to mask our conversation, I said, "I'm sorry about what Misha said."

"Don't be," he said, keeping his eyes on the screen. "I'm not."

Startled, I turned to look at his profile. His cheeks were slightly flushed.

"It was a lie," I said, probing cautiously. "Doesn't that bother you?"

Ashar looked down at his hands and then at me. "It's not the truth," he agreed. "Not yet."

Not yet? My cheeks were starting to redden too. Not yet? A strange, wild thumping started in my chest. Was I having a heart attack? We stared at each other, a million things unsaid, a million questions unasked.

"POPCORN?" My father shouted right above our heads and thumped a bowl down in between us, spilling a few kernels on the couch. Ashar jumped to his feet, visibly panicked. Appa glared at him.

I raised an eyebrow at his accusing expression. "Thanks Appa." He glared at me too and stormed off. I watched his dramatic exit before patting the couch again.

"Sit." Ashar was still shifting from one foot to the other, a light sheen of sweat coating his forehead.

"I think I should go." He looked nervously towards the kitchen. "Your father doesn't seem to want me here."

"I want you here."

The words hung between us. Ashar turned a bright, flaming red. Wow. Was he going to spontaneously combust?

He sat down with a large thump. I bounced on the couch when his weight landed beside me. A giggle escaped me, the sound surprising both of us.

Ashar smiled, a tentative, hesitant smile. I smiled back, my heart lightening. Even Appa, banging the fridge door in the other room, couldn't ruin the moment for me.

"I want to be here too," he muttered, his familiar scowl making its appearance again. It was adorable. I wanted to kiss it off his face. But that might have been too much for both the men in my life. One might set fire to the kitchen and the other would go up in flames.

"Could we change this stupid movie?" he asked, grumpily.

"No." I slid down so I could lean my head against the back of the couch. I stared up at the ceiling. It had a crack that snaked out towards one corner. How had I never noticed that before?

"You're not even watching it," Ashar groused.

I tilted my head to the side. "No, I'm not. But I'm watching you watch it."

He mimicked my head tilt. And just like that we were looking into each other's eyes. Looking and smiling. It was like I couldn't stop smiling. If someone had told me yesterday that I would be smiling like a dumbass today, I would have punched them in the face.

*But here I was. Smiling like a dumbass.*

The front door slammed open. I stopped smiling.

***

Ashar and I went for a walk to get away from the tense vibes at home. "Where do you live?" I asked him as we strolled along the dirty, crowded pavement.

"Close by." He shoved his hands into his pockets. "In Koramangala itself. It's practically walking distance."

"So, let's walk there?" I asked, curious to see what his house would be like, what his family would be like.

"Sure," he shrugged, his hands still stuffed inside his pockets.

How was I going to hold his hand if he kept them safely out of the way like that? I swung my arms vigorously on both sides, hoping he'd get the hint.

He hunched his shoulders and shifted away from me.

I swung my arms harder and smacked him in the face.

"Ow." He held his palm to one eye and glared at me from the other.

"Sorry." I shoved my hands into my own pockets and looked down at the road.

"We're here," he said, a minute later, stopping in front of a slightly older apartment building. What it lacked in pizazz, it made up for in class. Old, stately and just the teeniest bit shabby.

"I love it," I breathed.

"It's a building," he said, drily.

"It has character. It's vintage."

"Vintage?" he snorted. "What are you; a fifty-year-old lady?"

"Oh shut up!"

"Witty as always!" he laughed.

"Are we going to stand here forever? Or actually go in?"

"I don't know. Are you going to call my parents vintage?"

I growled.

"Okay. Okay." He held his hands up, palms out. "We'll go in."

He walked backwards into the building lift. "If you promise to growl at my sister like that, I would do anything you want?"

"Would you kiss me?"

He walked right into the lift wall. I winced at the loud crack when he hit the wall.

"I am so sorry."

He just shook his head as if to dislodge the ringing noise in his ears.

"Should I just go home? Before I kill you?"

It was a good thing he was laughing even while he sank to the floor, clutching his head. At least, that's what I am telling myself.

# Twenty-Two

## Misha

I stared at the counsellor's tastefully decorated walls. Pale blues and greens interspersed with white created a soothing, calming ambience.

If someone had truly asked me what I wanted to do with my life, it would have been this. No, not counselling, but interior decoration.

Instead, I'd chosen science and engineering out of spite. Mostly because I knew it would piss my mother off to see me following in my father's footsteps. She would see it as me choosing him over her. When it really was – just me not choosing her. Just the way she hadn't chosen me.

The counsellor walked in and Ma straightened herself in her seat. I watched the doctor walk over to the desk. She was younger than I'd expected. She smiled at me, sweetly. I made sure my trademark blank expression was in place. It didn't seem to faze her in the least.

I zoned out as Ma launched into a long, rambling explanation of why we were here. It went on for so long, I might as well have taken a short nap in between. The counsellor watched me, a small smile gracing her face every now and then. Was she even paying attention to Ma? She was currently listing all the different ways I made her life difficult.

"Mrs Banerjee," she cut in finally. "Could I speak to Misha alone? With your permission?"

Ma looked shocked to have been cut off mid-sentence. She caught her breath and nodded before rising to leave.

The door shut behind her with a quiet click. I watched the counsellor, warily. She took a notepad and wrote something in it that I couldn't see. Believe me, I tried but in vain.

"So, Misha." She shut the pad, looked at me and folded her hands. I stopped trying to crane my neck to get a look at her pad and slumped back in my seat. "Would you like to tell me why you're here?"

"My mother brought me." I slumped lower.

"And you don't want to be here," she said, sympathetically. "I hate being forced to do things too."

"Is this you trying to create a bond between us by pretending to be on my side?" I asked, sourly. She laughed. "Is it working?"

I smiled, reluctantly. "Not really."

"I am on your side, Misha." She sobered, quickly. "You are my patient. Not your mother or anyone else. There is only one side for me. Yours. And if you don't believe anything else I say, believe this. I will never be pretending."

I wanted to believe her. I did. But that familiar fatigue was cruising through me and I just wanted to be done with this. I wanted to go home and sleep for a few hours; or maybe forever. She was still watching me closely.

"I think today might have been too much for you with your earlier visit to the doctor and the tests that you've had to take. Can we schedule something next week?"

I nodded. It seemed easier to give in. The sooner I left, the sooner I could go to sleep.

Ma was allowed back in from her banishment. She darted looks from me to the counsellor like we were part of some secret club that had excluded her from it on purpose.

I would have been amused if I'd had had the energy for it. Instead, I just closed my eyes and shut them both out.

I heard them talking about a follow up appointment the coming Saturday.

"Misha." The counsellor's voice dragged me from my half slumber. "Does 11:00 a.m. on Saturday work for you?"

I shrugged. It seemed to be enough of an answer for both the adults.

"I'll see you then." The counsellor got to her feet, forcing us to ours as well.

Ma thanked her effusively. You would think the counsellor had already fixed her defective daughter. Nausea churned in my stomach again and I backed away from the scene before I threw up all over them. I truly was 'Pukey'.

***

*Hey babe … send me a nudie na?*

A wave of fury rose through the soul sucking fatigue I was swimming in. I'd told him I was going to the doctor today and that was all he thought to message me about? Bloody Ashar came running to spend the day with Katya just because she cried and all I got was requests for nude pictures.

I turned my phone off without answering and threw myself onto the bed. To hell with him and everyone else. I shut my eyes, wishing I could shut the world out as easily. But the world wouldn't go away so soon. It was still going to be waiting for me when I woke up. I willed myself to sleep, emptying my mind and calming my restless self. The dream when it came was so real, my living nightmare in technicolour glory.

*I was walking through the school, hurrying through the corridors. All around me kids ran towards their own classrooms.*

*Strangely, I didn't know any of them. I'd been a part of this school since Kindergarten. It was beyond odd that I wouldn't know anyone.*

*I was still puzzling through the slew of new faces when I realized I was lost. The corridor didn't look familiar. How could I be lost? I knew every inch of this school!*

*"Hey!" I tried to stop a younger boy walking past me. "How do I get to 10 C?"*

*He walked right past me like I didn't exist. What the hell was going on?*

*"Hey!!!" I shouted louder. Everyone around me just kept on walking. What the hell was going on?*

*A thin sheen of sweat broke out on my forehead. Something was wrong. Horribly, nauseatingly wrong. The now familiar churning in my stomach started and I slapped a hand over my mouth. I had to keep it in. I wasn't going to throw up in front of all these strange people who were already ignoring me, judging me and finding me lacking.*

*Someone shoved me from behind and I lost my balance. The churning got worse even as my head started to spin.*

*What was happening? Where was I? The corridor wasn't looking familiar anymore. Was I even at school?*

*Everyone was looking at me now. I was starting to panic. I was feeling hot and uncomfortably sweaty. I tried to open the top button on my uniform shirt but my hand only encountered sweaty, clammy skin.*

*I moved my hand around on my chest, even as I kept an eye on the creepy, staring kids around me. And felt nothing…*

*I looked down, my heart plummeting to the soles of my feet. I was stark naked!*

*"Aww babe." The slow drawl had my blood freezing. "You spoil me. All I asked for was a picture."*

*All around us kids were now laughing and pointing. I tried to cover myself with my hands knowing that it wasn't going to help.*

I woke up panting and gasping in my bed. My sheets were soaked with sweat. I threw myself out of the bed and landed on the floor. My back slammed against my study table. I barely felt the pain as I scrambled to my feet and rushed to the bathroom to splash some water on my face. But even the freezing cold water didn't do anything for the terror that seemed to seep into the very pores of my skin.

A knock sounded on my bedroom door. I started out of my thoughts still feeling disoriented and shaky.

"Misha? Dinner time." Uncle Kannan's quiet voice had me feeling strangely weepy.

"I'm not hungry," I replied without opening the door.

After a moment's silence, he said, "I'll have Sush bring you a dinner tray, just in case you change your mind later."

The gentleness in his voice was my undoing. I sank to the floor, one palm still on the door as if it would help me draw in his goodness, as if it would help soothe my fractured self. Tears streamed down my face. Endless, silent, painful.

But when I spoke, my voice was steady. Calm even.

"Thank you."

It was all I could manage for the moment.

# Twenty-Three

## Katya

Ashar and I spent the day lounging around in his bedroom, watching movies on his laptop and going through his bookshelf. His father was at work and his mother was surprisingly lenient when it came to allowing girls into his room.

I lay on my back and stared up at the ceiling. Was this what it felt like to have a normal home?

"Ashar baba?" The maid came in with a tray of sandwiches and juice. My stomach rumbled and Ashar laughed.

He bounded off the bed to take the tray and set it on his study table.

"Cheese and tomato or mint chutney?" he asked.

"Mint chutney, please." I took the plate with the sandwich on it and bit into it. The flavours erupted in my mouth making me sigh in pleasure. I'd been worried Aunty Sush had killed my taste buds. "You're acting like you don't get food at your house," Ashar laughed.

I grimaced. "I do. Most of the time it's not very good."

"Then learn to cook?" he suggested.

I rolled my eyes at him. "I'm a fairly decent cook, Mr Judgy."

"Then what's the problem?"

"I don't want to hurt Aunty Sush's feelings." I finished my sandwich and reached for a tomato one this time. "She's got this thing in her head that she needs to be this homemaker-cum-career-cum-professional-superwoman. And me volunteering

to cook would be the equivalent of jumping up and saying 'Hah. You suck. Me awesome. Me feed family now'."

"You're a clown," he said, affectionately. "But a sweet one."

He took a sip of his juice and watched me thoughtfully. "Misha is going to eat you alive."

I stiffened. "I can hold my own."

"There are things you don't know yet about them."

"About the Vipers?"

"The Vipers?" Ashar looked startled. "Is that what they're calling themselves now?"

"Oh that! Bhavya and I came up with it," I said, feeling more than a little proud of my friend and myself.

Until Ashar started to laugh. And didn't stop.

"Why are you cackling like a hyena?"

A petite girl with long, beautiful hair walked in and glared at Ashar.

"I can't practice my singing with all this noise." She looked like she wanted to stamp her foot in frustration but she noticed me and controlled herself.

"Are you Ashar's girlfriend?" She tilted her head to one side, her waist length hair sliding over one shoulder with the movement.

"Umm, ahh," I babbled.

"Katya, this is my nosy sister Sehar. She's a budding singer and…"

"I am not a budding singer," Sehar informed me loftily, interrupting Ashar. "I am fully bloomed."

Ashar snorted. "Go to your room and screech. Katya and I are busy."

"Busy doing what?" Sehar waggled her eyebrows suggestively.

Ashar groaned. "You're ten years old. Act your damn age."

"You're fifteen," she said sweetly. "Too young to lose your virginity no?"

"That's it. Out!" Ashar shoved her out of the room and shut the door in her face.

"I'm so sorry about that," he mumbled, his ears going red again.

I giggled. "Well, I'd say she's a million times better than my so-called sibling."

"I hate to break it to you," Ashar said, wryly. "That's true for most people."

# Twenty-Four

## Misha

As I ran another lap around the school track field, I let my lungs expand and contract with each deep breath. One of the few times I felt like I had my life under control was when I was exercising. Yoga and track at school kept me sane.

I was so grateful I didn't have to see Katya's face in track practice anymore. I needed some space in my life to be devoid of my twisted, blended family.

I continued to run long after the coach blew his whistle and others stopped. It was the last period of the day and there was nowhere I could be. Nowhere but here.

And so, I ran and ran and ran until my legs gave way beneath me and I sank to the ground. My breath escaped me in harsh, hard pants. My legs quivered like jelly. But my mind had never been clearer.

I saw him standing by the edge of the playground. Waiting for me. He'd always had this terrible stillness in the way he stood. I hadn't seen it in anyone else. And that's why even from a distance, I knew who was standing there, waiting for me. And that's why I ran. But no matter how far I ran or how fast I ran, I could never run from him. Or from my memories.

All round, kids streamed past with their backpacks, thrilled to be done with another school day. I wished I could keep running but my body wouldn't let me move another muscle. So I sat in the dirt and watched him walk up to me. The microscopic speck in the distance got bigger and bigger until finally, he was towering over me.

"Hello Misha."

I squinted up at him. "Heylos Pops. It's nice to finally see you."

He stared at me. "Get up."

I grinned, the snarky, mocking grin he hated. I had it down pat. I stood up, not bothering to dust the muck off me.

"Your wish is my command." I sketched a bow that had his already pursed lips tightening. I knew exactly which buttons to push with my father and I didn't hesitate to use a sledgehammer on them.

"We need to talk." He started to walk away, confident that I would follow like an obedient, little puppy.

I dug my heels in and waited for him to realise I wasn't anywhere near him. He turned and marched back to me. I saw a couple of twelfth graders eyeing him as they walked past. My father was, much to my disgust, 'A Hot Dad'. I was used to people, especially women, swooning over him wherever we went.

"What is it?" he asked, tersely.

"I need to collect my things from class." I held my arms out. "And clean up before I can go anywhere."

"I'll be waiting for you in the car park." He strode off, without waiting for my reply. God forbid, anyone who didn't do as he commanded.

I took my own sweet time gathering my things and sauntering over to the parking lot where my father stood, his arms folded and a formidable glower on his face. He looked like a vengeful God.

"Does Ma know you are here?" I decided to fire the opening shot. "I don't need your mother's permission to see you," he said, getting into the driver's seat.

"Actually." I slid in through the passenger door. "You kinda do. She has custody of me. Remember custody? That thing you didn't want?"

His hands clenched around the steering wheel although he managed to flick a look at me that managed to convey his utter boredom and disdain all rolled into one glare.

"You're sixteen years old Misha. Try and act your age."

"Fifteen." The demon inside me wouldn't calm down. "You would know that if you remembered when my birthday is."

The car rolled to a stop at a traffic light. My father aka Mr Sperm Donor glared straight ahead.

"Enough, Misha." His fingers clenched on the steering wheel again. I was worried for the poor thing. It was being mangled. "Don't open your mouth till we reach."

I wanted to ask where we were going but that would qualify as opening my mouth. So, I shrugged and stared out of the window.

When we pulled into the entrance to a café and I saw my mother sitting at a table, I knew I was being ambushed. Whatever they had planned, it couldn't be good. I squared my shoulders, held my head high and marched onto the battlefield.

"Hey Mommy." I beamed at her, adding an eyelash flutter for no good reason. "It's so good to see Pops and you together after so long."

I turned the chair around and straddled it. Leaning forward, I winked slyly. "Does Uncle Kannan know you're having an affair again?"

When she stared at me, horrified, I mimicked her expression, holding my hands to my cheeks for additional effect.

"He doesn't know, does he?" I put a finger to my lips and whispered, "Don't worry. It will be our little secret."

"But honestly, Ma," I continued. "First you're married to Pops here and having an affair with Uncle Kannan. Then you marry him and have an affair with Pops. It's all very confusing. Is it so hard to make up your mind about whom you want?"

My mother shot my father a look. "See? I told you she's out of control."

He grunted. "And whose fault is that?"

"You're blaming me?" she shrieked. Several people in the café glanced over at our table.

"You have custody of her. You're supposed to be the one teaching her things."

Things? I'm amused that they think either of them is in a position to teach me anything.

"You didn't even want the responsibility of shared custody." My mother was in her lawyer mode now. "Where do you get off judging me? I'm doing the best I can."

I turned my head to my father for his next salvo. This is almost as much fun as watching Wimbledon. But instead of firing back, my father swung towards me.

"What is your problem? Why are you making life difficult for us?"

"How exactly am I making life difficult? Especially for you?" I couldn't resist adding the last bit.

The man hadn't been in touch for the last one year. How exactly could I have made his life difficult? If he could give me some tips on how to, I'd do my best to make his life living hell even from afar.

"Enough," he roared. He turned towards my mother. "You have spoilt her. All this counselling and stuff is just an excuse to waste money on her. She is a spoilt brat who thinks she can get her way by behaving like this."

A hesitant waitress walked up to us. "Sir, I'm afraid I'll have to ask you all to keep it down or leave. The other customers are getting disturbed."

My father clenched his jaw, a nerve ticking in his temple. He looked like he would explode at any moment. My mother reassured the waitress that we wouldn't be noisy anymore and quickly placed an order for a pizza and three lemonades. The waitress left but not without shooting worried glances at us over her shoulder.

"I hope you guys are going to leave a big tip for her," I drawled.

"That's it." This time it was my mother who lost her patience. These two were almost too easy to get a rise out of.

"Misha, I want to talk to you about something."

"Are you getting married again?" I couldn't resist the snide jibe. If looks could kill, my mother would be cremating me right now. "If you don't get your act together, we're going to send you off to boarding school."

Despite all my bravado, the words landed like a rock against my heart. Other parents would be trying to reach out to their kids, to try and find a way to mend the relationship. All mine wanted was to get rid of me.

I'm the problem that didn't fit anywhere. I didn't fit into their old life and I certainly didn't fit into their new lives either.

Tears brimmed inside me but I would be damned if I was going to let them see it trickle out. I gritted my teeth and forced a smile.

"Is being sent away from both of you supposed to be a punishment? It sounds more like you're rewarding me."

The pizza arrived at that moment. We sat in frozen silence as the waitress set it on the table along with the drinks.

The minute she left, my father turned to my mother. "I'm sick of her. Let her finish this year at St. Thomas and then she can go to boarding school. Find one that suits us."

"Even that I have to do?" My mother erupted. "You'll snap out orders and I will jump to obey?"

I served myself a slice of pizza and proceeded to eat it slowly as they argued. I'd learned early on in life to go about my routine even as they fought like cats and dogs around me. If I had waited for them to stop fighting, I would have starved to death.

*I'm sick of her.*

I forced the tears back and started on my second slice of pizza.

# Twenty-Five

## Katya

I came home from Math tuition to viciously uncomfortable vibes. Rock music blared from Misha's bedroom; so loudly that it was a wonder that the neighbours hadn't called the cops yet. It still didn't drown out the sounds of the fight my father and her mother were having in their bedroom.

What the hell had I missed? Clearly it wasn't going to be Blended movie night. It seemed more like a horror show.

"I don't care, Sush," my father shouted. "You were wrong."

I stopped on the landing, staring at their closed door in shock. My father was shouting? *My father?*

I couldn't hear whatever Aunty Sush said, her volume was too low. I scampered across the landing and into my room before anyone opened their door and saw me eavesdropping. If my father was shouting, then the end of the world was near. Better to stay out of the way.

The shouting and music went on until late at night. Nobody seemed interested in dinner that night, but my stomach was growling. I wasn't sure if it was safe to leave my room but unless I planned to start eating my pillows, I was going to have to brave the natives.

An eerie silence emanated from the older folk's bedroom. Misha's bedroom still had music playing but she'd moved on to Taylor Swift and at the same loud volume. I tiptoed down the stairs and to the kitchen. A peanut butter sandwich should be quick and easy to make and I could escape back to my room without meeting anyone.

I came to an abrupt halt a second later when I saw a butt protruding out of the open fridge. Oh shit! Of all the people to run into, it would have to be the Wicked Witch of Bengaluru.

The butt seemed to be swaying to Taylor's beat, which could be heard clearly all the way down here in the kitchen. I started to slowly back away before she emerged from the depths of the fridge. I would rather eat the pillows than listen to her insult me right now.

"There is nothing to eat." Her disembodied voice reached me just as I reached the threshold of the kitchen.

I froze. So much for escaping without notice.

"Unless." Her head emerged, eyes skewering me in place. "You want to try my mother's so-called mutton roganjosh?"

I shuddered. The fancier Aunty Sush's cooking got, the worse it tasted.

"I was thinking of a peanut butter sandwich," I said.

But Misha was already shaking her head. "I checked for that. No bread. We could share what's left of the peanut butter if you want."

Share? Misha was going to share food with me?? Was my share poisoned? Did I even want to eat with her after what she'd done?

"Or." Her eyes brightened. My stomach sank even further. "I found a bottle of Coke and a tub of ice cream."

Ice cream and Coke for dinner? With Misha? This whole evening had taken on a surreal quality. Maybe I was still asleep and this was all a dream?

A loud fizzing sound told me I was wide awake.

"Either come in or get out," Misha snapped.

Ahh, there she was. The Misha I knew.

I came in.

Misha uncapped the tub of Baskin Robbins Mint Choco Chip and I pulled out glasses and bowls and spoons for the two of us.

We carted everything to the dining table and spread it out. It turned out to be a regular feast. We were going to be bouncing off the walls with all this sugar in our system.

"Have you heard the good news yet?" Misha asked, licking her spoon clean of ice cream.

"Good news?" I froze. What good news? Was she pregnant? Was that why she kept vomiting?

"You only have to tolerate me for a couple more months." She threw her arms out like she was ecstatic but the expression on her face didn't mirror the pose.

I put my spoon down. "What do you mean?"

"My parents are shipping their biggest burden off to boarding school. You don't have to live with the girl you hate anymore."

"Now?" I was shocked.

"Don't be daft." She rolled her eyes. "After we're done with tenth grade. Who is going to give me admission now?"

I stared at her. Boarding school?

"Do you want to go?"

Misha laughed. There was zero humour in that sound.

"Do you know," she said, waving her spoon at me. "You're probably the only person to ask me that question."

"I'm sorry, Misha," I said, a strange ache building up in my chest. I didn't like her but I wouldn't wish her to be banished either.

"Why?" She slugged her Coke down. "You're not the one throwing me out of your life. Unless, you had something to do with their decision?"

"Of course not!" I was horrified that she would think something like that.

Misha snickered. "You are such an easy mark."

I flushed.

"Is that why you did what you did?" I asked, quietly.

She froze, the spoon in her mouth.

"I don't know what you mean," she said, finally.

"Yes, you do," I countered. "You're many things but you're not a coward. What did you get out of it?"

She stared at me as if she was seeing me for the first time. I stared back. I wasn't the girl she'd first met. I wasn't going to run from a showdown just because she was bigger, meaner and crueler. Or maybe I was just braver with so much sugar inside me.

"I don't know." Her voice was quiet, contemplative, even a little sad. "I don't know why I do some of the things I do. I can't help myself sometimes."

"Does it make you feel better?" I asked, curious to know what pushed her to do this.

She dug her spoon into her ice cream and stared at it. "No. No, it doesn't. But if it hadn't been you that day, it would have been me."

"Wow." I was stunned at the selfishness in that sentence. "At least you're honest."

She looked at me then, something desperate and bitter in her eyes. "You wouldn't understand."

"No, I wouldn't." I didn't really want to talk anymore.

We ate our way through our sugar binge in silence for a bit. Vague noises drifted down from upstairs.

"The parentals are arguing again," Misha remarked.

I shot a nervous look towards the stairs.

"I don't know what they're fighting about," I murmured. "I've never heard them fight like this before."

"Me," she said, matter of factly. "They're fighting about me."

"The boarding school thing?" I wasn't surprised. My father would have been furious over that. He kept his family and friends close and his kids in his pocket. That he considered Misha one of his own was never in doubt. Appa didn't know how not to love.

"He probably won't let it happen."

Misha snorted. "Your father is no match for the combined might of my parents."

"You'd be surprised at what my father is capable of." My eyes strayed to the stairs again. The argument was getting louder. "When he feels strongly enough about something, he's a force to be reckoned with."

# Twenty-Six

## Misha

*Send me a nudie!*

I stared at Samar's message. No matter how many times I checked it, the content didn't change. The pit in my stomach deepened. He was relentless.

*Are you drunk? How long are you going to keep this up?*

I waited to see what response my message would get but there was only silence. I flopped back on my bed, my mind running in a million different directions. Maybe boarding school wasn't such a bad idea after all. I could get away from everything. And everyone! My stomach was churning with that mixture of coke and ice cream. Or was it churning because of Samar's request.

I stared at my phone. Still silent. Was he angry?

Sweat beaded my forehead. Of course he was angry. This was Samar. He thought he could get whatever he wanted, whenever he wanted.

And was I going to give him what he wanted? I bolted from the bed and made it to the bathroom just in time for the ice cream to make an ungainly exit.

The back of my throat burned as my so-called dinner came flying out of my mouth. Shit! Was that stupid stomach flu back? Was I having a relapse? Or was I really bulimic?

I was still heaving and retching over the toilet bowl when someone entered my bedroom. I groaned at the sound of the footsteps. I wasn't up for any more interaction with any of them.

"Misha?" Katya's concerned voice reached me in the depths of my misery. "Bathroom." I managed to gasp before collapsing on the floor beside the toilet.

"Oh shit." She rushed into the bathroom. "What the hell happened?"

"I guess ice cream for dinner was a bad idea." I tried to make a joke but neither of us were laughing.

"Come on." She slipped her arm under my shoulder and heaved me up. "Let's get you cleaned up."

We flushed the toilet without directly looking at its contents. I rinsed my mouth and brushed my teeth. Katya hovered nearby. Probably to catch me if I fainted like a Victorian maiden.

Once I was back in bed, she said, "I'll go get Aunty Sush."

"Why?" I asked, even as a small part of me whined for my mother. Whined silently, I might add.

Katya looked confused. "She should know you're not well. She'll help you feel better. Give you medicines and stuff."

I laughed, a rough bark of sound. "Don't tell her. I don't need any more of her drama right now."

Katya hesitated, obviously torn between doing the right thing and doing what I was asking of her. Poor Kitty Cat. She was such a good girl.

Something struck me as I watched her chew her lip and shift from one foot to the other in the doorway.

"Why did you come to my room?" I asked, curiously. This had never happened before. "Was there something you needed?" It was like I'd flipped a switch. All the colour leached out of her face.

"What?" I sat up in bed. "What is it?"

"Have you checked your social media?"

Ice slid through my veins. "Not in the last half an hour. Why?"

She pulled her phone out of her pocket and held it out to me. "You should check out Samar's latest post."

The ice cracked a little. Of course.

Katya sat next to me and laid a hand on my thigh. I flinched away from the contact. I didn't need her pity. I didn't need anyone's pity. I didn't need anyone.

I swiped my phone and tapped on the social media. Samar's latest post was right at the top of my feed.

345 likes, 53 comments. The numbers continued to climb even as I watched.

*The love of my life.*

The reel that accompanied the caption was a montage of my pictures. Pouty, kissing faces … he'd included a lot of the pictures I'd shared just with him or he had clicked of me. Which wouldn't have been too bad if he hadn't ended it with that one.

It was a split second and it was just a glimpse but you could see that I was topless. Samar had obviously taken a screenshot that day.

Shit. My parents were going to kill me.

This time when Katya wrapped an arm around my waist, I didn't flinch away. I leaned in.

***

The whispers started as soon as I entered school the next morning. Boys grinning, girls smirking and worst of all, Samar. He sat in his regular seat, the expression on his face of a victor enjoying his spoils. I stood at the front of the class and stared at him.

This was the first boy I'd ever had a crush on. I still remembered the day he'd told me he'd liked me too. Halfway through seventh grade, he'd stopped me outside of music class with a cheesy handmade card. We'd spent that lunch hour, holding hands under the cafeteria table and whispering to each other.

He'd been the one to smuggle in pads for me when I'd got my period at school unexpectedly. He'd held me as I sobbed through my parent's divorce. He'd sat by my hospital bed, after my appendix was removed, and walked me through the lessons I was missing.

How had we gone from that to this? What had changed? When did we change? When did we become these people? Who played power games to stay together, who hurt each other more than we loved each other?

Why did I still want him in my life?

"Misha," Kukkad snapped from behind. "Are you going to stand in the entrance of the classroom and daydream the whole day?"

I flushed as the class erupted in snickers. Katya started to rise from her seat but I glared at her. She sat back down.

This was my battle and nobody else would fight it. Ice cream bonding, notwithstanding.

I strode past the giggling, smirking rows and sat down in my regular seat beside Samar.

"Hey babe," he said, his arm slung across the back of his seat.

The depth of the rage that surged inside me startled me. Samar had been my one constant all these years. The two of us, our equation as the most popular couple in school, our social standing … this was all I had. And now, he was taking that away from me too.

I ignored his greeting and concentrated on getting my books out. On his other side, Malu smirked at me. She must be enjoying this moment more than anybody else. She should make the most of it because it wasn't going to last very long.

Kukkad droned on in the background but my mind was on what I had to do next. It was my fault, wasn't it?

I should not have taken my shirt off. I shouldn't have opened myself up to the possibility of something like this happening. I shouldn't have continued loving Samar long after he had stopped being lovable.

"Why did you do it?" I turned to him, my abrupt movement causing his hand to slide off my chair.

"What?" he asked, shooting a wary look towards Kukkad who thankfully was writing something on the blackboard and hadn't heard us.

"You know what." I was tired of his games and I was, more importantly, tired of playing along. "Why did you post a topless picture of me on social media?"

I didn't realise my voice had risen. Nor did I notice that the whole class including Kukkad were staring at us. I was only watching Samar, desperately hoping to see something on his face. Shame, guilt, regret … anything, anything at all that could salvage our relationship and redeem him.

He smirked instead, amusement lighting up his eyes. "Don't worry … I edited it before putting it up. Made them," his glance slid down to my breasts, "look better."

I was numb. For one second, I didn't feel anything. I didn't hear anything. And most importantly, I didn't say anything.

And then the dam broke.

I slapped him. The sound rang through the otherwise silent classroom. It was hard enough to send him tumbling back into Malu who in turn, fell backwards and on to the floor. I grabbed my bag and walked out, ignoring my staring classmates and shocked teacher.

I started to run the minute I left the classroom. I didn't stop running until I reached the tree at the end of the playground. Huddled behind its large trunk and out of sight of the other children, I slumped on to a bench, wrapped my hands around my bent legs and let go.

The sobs racked my body, shame, guilt, anger, hurt – a toxic cocktail spewing out of me. I curled myself into a tighter ball but it did nothing to lessen the pain.

Someone wrapped their arms around me. I wanted to shrug it off but it had been so long since someone had touched me to offer comfort that I didn't have it in me to pull away. So I turned into the embrace and held on.

# Twenty-Seven

## Katya

I held Misha as she cried like her heart was breaking. It probably was but until today, I hadn't really thought she had a heart. I mentally squashed that mean, spiteful thought like a grape and concentrated on holding on to her. And to my sanity. What the hell was going to happen now?

My anxiety was sitting up and doing a tribal dance in my chest. And Misha was soaking through my shirt with her tears. She cried actual tears. Imagine that! I was too used to her shooting lightning bolts from her eyes.

Misha was starting to wind down. I continued to rub her back in slow, small circles, just the way Appa does when he's trying to comfort me.

"Stop it," she moaned. "You're making me nauseous."

My hand froze in mid circle.

"Sorry," I muttered. "I thought I was helping."

She sat up, wiping her eyes. "You are," she sighed. "I just can't handle the constant motion. Makes me feel a bit seasick."

"On land?" My eyebrows shot up. This was the weirdest thing I'd ever heard. Misha snorted, the sound a mix between irritation and amusement. On the plus side, she wasn't crying anymore.

"Are you okay?" I asked.

"Do I look okay?" she snapped back.

"Well, you're being mean again. So yeah, I think you're okay."

She laughed. A genuine belly laugh that had me grinning too.

Our smiles faded a moment later as we watched Ashar walk over to us. “Here comes trouble,” Misha muttered. I couldn’t argue with that. Ashar did look like trouble from the scowl on his face to the slouch and clenched fists. Delicious trouble.

I wanted to snuggle up and… “You’re required in the principal’s office.” His words dumped a bucket of ice water on my head.

“Me?” I squeaked.

“Not you, doofus.” He rolled his eyes at me. “You.” I followed his pointed finger towards Misha.

“Why does she have to go the principal’s office? Samar is the dick who screwed up.” I was on my feet, outrage making me squeaky again.

“You can argue that with Princi.” He rocked on his heels. “Please use the same words too.” I stuck my tongue out at him. “So mature.” He shook his head at me and looked over at Misha. “I think you should get there soon.”

She took a deep breath. “I don’t want to go.”

“I don’t think they’re asking for a vote on it,” Ashar said, sympathetically. “They’ve called Samar in also and…”

“And?” I asked, when he just shifted uncomfortably from one foot to the other.

“And both sets of parents.” The blood drained out of Misha’s face. “Boarding school, here I come,” she muttered.

“It’s not your fault,” I reminded her. “Samar is the one who is in the wrong.”

“Don’t fool yourself, Kitty Cat.” Her sardonic tone stung. “He isn’t going to take the fall for this with me and definitely won’t take it alone either.”

***

I watched Misha walk away from us, her shoulders back, nose and eyes red. Say what you will about her, she had a spine of steel. I snuck a sideways glance at Ashar who was also watching Misha walk towards the admin block.

"That asshole has a lot to answer for," he murmured, his delicious scowl back.

I sighed. If only life was a bit more like a novel, then Samar would be expelled, Misha would be nicer, Ashar would fall in love with me, Amma would be alive … the possibilities were endless.

But this wasn't fiction. This was real life. Which meant Amma was never coming back, Misha would probably be the one getting expelled and shipped off to boarding school, Samar would be back on campus to torment us all after a token suspension and Ashar … Ashar would still be standing around, scowling, with his hands jammed in his pockets.

How could I ever hold hands with him if he always kept them buried in his pants? Stupid fellow. Why was such a simple thing so hard for him to understand?

I shifted awkwardly beside him as the bell rang and kids spewed out of all the classrooms.

"I guess we should get back," I said when he continued to stare in the direction Misha had disappeared to.

"Do you know I once had a crush on her?" His abrupt question had me stumbling even though I hadn't started to move yet.

"What?" I gaped at him. "Come again! What??"

"Misha. We were the best of friends since kindergarten and then in eighth grade I developed the most inconvenient crush on her."

"Inconvenient?" The word felt clunky on my tongue.

"Yes." He laughed. "Because she didn't like me back. She liked my friend."

"Samar." I seemed to only be able to speak in single word sentences. He nodded, a bitter, twisted expression on his face. "He was my friend. He was until…"

Until? Until what? This was like watching a daily soap that ended on a cliffhanger. Except, the hero I'd hoped was mine was in love with my somewhat-sister. It was like being stabbed in the heart with a red hot poker.

"I don't know what changed. I don't know when he changed. But suddenly, I wasn't cool enough for them. I wasn't rich enough and I think even my name wasn't socially acceptable enough."

I flinched. So many things made sense now. Ashar's initial animosity towards me. His anger, his silence, his avoidance. It all made sense now. What a fool I was! How had I thought he liked me?

"We should help her." He was still glaring fiercely at the school building. "Samar shouldn't get away with what he did."

"Why would he get away with it?" I asked, my first full sentence since Ashar had started speaking.

He turned disbelieving eyes on me. "You don't know why?"

"Clearly I don't know anything," I shot back bitterly. "Don't stop enlightening me now."

He looked a little startled by my reaction but he did. "His father is a big time politician. If anyone is going to get into trouble today, it's Misha, not him."

Misha. Misha. Misha.

I felt like my head would explode each time he uttered her name. How had I not seen this? How had I thought, even for a minute, that he liked me?

Uncontrollable rage swirled through me. I'd always done the right thing. I'd always been the good girl. And what had it got me? Nothing.

I was always the one on the losing side. And Misha ... she'd done nothing but taunt, torment and torture everyone around her, including me. And ... Okay. So she wasn't exactly on the winning side at the moment. But she had been. So many times. So many, many times. It wasn't fair that she should get my guy too. Except that apparently he'd been her guy all along.

"Are you going to help her?" Ashar was like a dog with a bone.

"Why don't you?" I exploded. "Since it obviously means so much to you. *She* obviously means so much to you."

"Are you mad?" He yelled right back. "Or just selfish?"

"Selfish?" I was screeching now. The other kids were starting to turn and stare. "I am selfish? Misha, the love of your life, is the most selfish, self centered one I've ever come across."

"OMG, Katya. Are you for real right now?" He shook his head, disbelievingly. "This is not about you. None of this is about you."

No, of course it isn't. It was never about me. It was always about someone else. My father's happiness. Aunty Sush's selfishness. Misha's meanness. Ashar's crush.

None of it was ever about me. "Are you going to help her or no?" Ashar exploded. I didn't bother answering him. If no one else was going to bother about me, I would.

# Twenty-Eight

## Misha

I stared at my feet as I sat in the Principal's room waiting for the parents to stop arguing. Samar's parents were outraged by my accusations and my mother was outraged that her daughter was caught in the high school version of a sex scandal.

A gentle touch had me starting out of my deep introspection of my dirty school shoes. Uncle Kannan squeezed my shoulders and moved his chair closer to mine. I blinked back the sudden sting of tears.

"Our son has done nothing wrong," Samar's mother declared. "That middle class girl is the one who has created all this tamasha for nothing."

"Middle class?" My mother drew in a deep, offended breath. "Middle class???" This time it was close to a shriek.

Uncle Kannan sighed. "Sush, please. That's not what is important right now." He turned to face the Principal. "Misha has told us what has happened. I'd like to know what you plan to do about it."

Principal Meenakshi Verma looked very uncomfortable. Her crisp, starched light blue cotton saree was starting to wilt in the heat, just like her composure. She cleared her throat and looked at the angry parents.

"I think we must ascertain the true facts first," she said, finally. "Can I see Samar's social media profile please? I would like to see this video."

"You can't," the sullen ass responded. "There is no such video."

My head snapped up. "You're a bloody liar." I pulled my phone out and opened it to Samar's profile on social media. I handed the Principal my phone.

She looked down and scrolled for a second before looking up. "I can't see anything like what you mentioned here, Misha. Could you show me?" I took the phone back and stared at the screen disbelievingly. The snake had obviously deleted it. From the corner of my eye, I saw him smirk.

"Principal Ma'am, I told you, I didn't do anything like that. She's making it up."

"I am not!" A hot, burning sensation spread across my chest. "I am telling the truth."

"Oh Misha." My mother gave a long suffering sigh.

"He's deleted it." I whirled round to face her. "Surely, you know that's possible. Ask any of the kids in class. They've all seen it."

The principal cleared her throat again. "We did ask all the children in your class. They said they didn't know what you were talking about. In fact," she consulted some notes on her pad. "Your friend Mallika said this wasn't the first time you'd made this kind of a baseless accusation." The burning sensation spread to my face. "Why would I do that?"

"Because you like attention?" Principal Verma looked at me, a slight flush creeping up her cheeks. She believed me. She knew what she was doing was wrong. And yet, Samar's father's money and clout were enough to make her shame me.

"I'm sure cybercrime can retrieve the video once we make a complaint." Uncle Kannan's steely voice cut through.

"Cybercrime?" Samar's father's blustery voice cut through. "Now look here. I won't let you ruin my son's future and our family's reputation on your characterless daughter's baseless allegations."

"There is nothing for you to let or to not let. I will do what I need to do for my daughter's sake and I hope," he looked pointedly at the principal. "So will the school."

She shifted uncomfortably in her chair. "Well, without proof, I can't take any action. It's her word against his."

"And you believe him?" Uncle Kannan rose from his chair, the most unlikely avenging angel. "Well, I believe my daughter. I will go to cybercrime and bring you the proof you need. You better be ready to take action after that."

My eyes overflowed. He believed me! He called me his daughter! "Oh let it be, Kannan." My mother's tired voice cut through. "You know what Misha is like. She must have made it up."

"I didn't!"

"Shut up, Misha." Ma stood up. "Let's go home."

"See!" Samar's mother said, triumphantly. "Even her mother knows what kind of girl she is."

My entire body went numb. Everyone was standing in preparation to leave.

"One moment, Misha." The principal also stood. "I'm afraid I'll have to suspend you for a week from school. We can't have you spreading lies and slander like this."

"You cannot suspend her!" Uncle Kannan looked like he'd explode with rage.

"Yes, I can," she said, firmly. "For making accusations without proof and for spreading malicious lies."

"And what if there is proof?" The new voice had us all turning to the door.

Katya walked in and took her place beside her father.

***

For a moment, nobody moved and then everybody started talking at once.

"Who is this girl now?" Samar's father demanded.

"My other daughter," Uncle Kannan said, tersely.

"Oh God. One more liar to listen to," the man sneered.

Uncle Kannan looked ready to explode. Katya laid a calming hand on his arm.

"This liar has proof," she said, turning to face the principal.

"What proof?" the principal asked, uneasily, her plans for a neat resolution to this mess crumbling in front of her eyes.

"I have screenshots of everything Samar has posted. I reported it on social media as did some friends of mine." Katya's calm speech had everyone in the room shrinking into themselves.

"My friends and I have seen the posts and are more than willing to speak up about it to anyone who asks. I'm sure cybercrime would want to know. Also, Appa," she said, turning to Uncle Kannan. "I'm sure cybercrime officers can retrieve the data even if he has deleted it for now."

She pulled out her phone and scrolled through till she found what she was looking for.

"The screenshots I spoke about." She handed her phone to the principal. "I have them backed up in case they get accidentally deleted," she added mildly.

"What are you trying to imply?" Principal Verma bristled.

"Nothing, Ma'am," Katya said, meekly. "It's just that sometimes our finger slips. Always good to have some security in place."

Silence descended on the room as the principal stared at the phone. My heart thudded so loudly in my chest that I thought everyone could hear it. But no one looked at me. They were all staring at the principal.

Finally, she sighed and looked up. "Samar, you're suspended from the school indefinitely until further investigation of this matter."

"How dare you?" Samar's father's roar was deafening. "I will have you removed from that post by the end of the day."

"I'm sure you will," she said, facing him squarely. "And then all this nonsense will be the headache of my replacement."

"Am I still suspended?" I asked, wondering if I truly cared.

She stared at me for a moment. "Yes," she said. "You created a ruckus in class and disrupted classes for the day. You have physically attacked a classmate when you should have brought this matter to the notice of an adult so that appropriate action could be taken. You are still suspended until the end of the week."

And because I was the reason she might lose her job, I thought bitterly. I nodded and turned to leave. Uncle Kannan stopped me with a hand on my shoulder.

"One minute, Misha," he said. He turned to face the room. "We accept your decision with regard to her suspension but there is one more matter to attend to."

He wrapped an arm around my shoulders. "I believe you owe my child an apology for doubting her. And we would like that now please."

I burst into tears. Big, noisy sobs that had everyone backing away from me.

Uncle Kannan only drew me closer.

"Now! Or you can apologise when cybercrime officers knock on your door."

"Samar, apologise," his father said.

"What?" It was the first time he'd spoken since Katya walked in. "I'm not apologising to that two-faced witch."

A loud crack resounded through the room as his father slapped him. He stumbled back into his mother's arms, shocked and silent.

I could see his cheek reddening with his father's handprint. A tinge of sympathy swept through my heart as I watched him.

"Apologise to her and to us for putting us through the humiliation of this moment." The soft snarl had me backing up. Uncle Kannan tightened his hold on my shoulders keeping me in place.

"I'm s-s-sorry," Samar stuttered, tears flowing down his face.

I'd never seen him cry before.

His father came around and stood in front of Uncle Kannan with folded hands. Ever the perfect politician. He'd obviously decided to take a different track now. Maybe our principal wouldn't lose her job.

"I am very sorry about what my son has done. I apologise on behalf of our family. It will not happen again."

Uncle Kannan gave him a stiff nod. I couldn't hold his gaze.

He gathered his family and prepared to leave.

"You might want to ask yourselves one question though," Samar's father said from where he stood near the door.

"How did my son get that picture of your daughter?"

# Twenty-Nine

## Katya

"I'm proud of you, Kitty." Appa said as he sat down beside me on my bed. He seemed to have showered and changed into his trademark white kurta pyjama. His familiar Cinthol deodorant wafted around the room. I'd tried to get him to change to something cooler and more fashionable but he wouldn't budge from his old, tried and tested habits.

Today, all I wanted was to bury myself in that familiar smell and hold on tight.

"Appa," I said holding on to his chest. "I hate it here. I want to go home."

He didn't answer but his arms tightened around me. After a while, he said, "Home is wherever the two of us are together, Kitty. There is no home left in Coimbatore to go back to. I'm sorry you've been so unhappy with this shift. It's my fault. I should have discussed things with you before making all these big decisions. Meena would be so disappointed in me if she could see what a mess I've made of things."

I snorted. "Amma forgave you every time. I don't think she knew how to be disappointed in you."

"And you, Kitty? Will you forgive me?"

"Appa, don't be silly." I snuggled in closer. "There is nothing to forgive."

"Yes, there is." He brought my hand to his lips and kissed it. "Misha told me everything."

"Everything?" I sat up in bed, pushing away from his embrace. "What is everything?"

"About how she was mean to you, how she bullied you, the problems you had in school with that Samar boy and even about them making fun of your nickname."

I took a deep breath. Misha hadn't told him about what they'd done with my mother's picture, had she? I shoved the panic aside and tried to speak as calmly as possible. "It's not a big deal. Usual ragging and stuff. Misha and Samar are the popular kids in school and they tease the less popular ones like me. That's all."

"She told me about what they did with your picture with Amma and the sleazy way they twisted your pet name."

My heart cracked. "They had no right to do what they did," I gulped, tears streaming down my face. "They used Amma and what she called me and they…"

He held me close and let me sob my heart out into his chest.

"I miss her so much," I wailed. "I want her to come back."

"I know, baby. I know. I miss her too." He wiped his own tears.

"I will never forgive Misha for what she did that day." I scrubbed my face as my sobs slowly slowed.

"And yet, you helped her." He was watching me closely.

I didn't respond. I almost hadn't. I'd been so upset by what Ashar had told me that I wanted Misha to suffer. I wanted her to know what it felt like to be me, to have things go against you even when you tried so hard. But I couldn't do it. If that made me a loser, then so be it.

I shrugged, realizing my father was still watching me.

"Why did you take screenshots of that post?" he asked.

I sighed. I'd known this was coming. I wondered if I could get away with some noble, brave reason but in the end I decided to go with the truth.

"Ammunition," I said, resignedly. "In case she got me into trouble at a later date and I needed something to use against her."

"Well it certainly was useful," Appa mused. "Except that you didn't use it against her but for her."

"I know! What a waste," I grumbled. He laughed and ruffled my hair. "You'll have time to gather more ammunition over the years."

"Not if she's sent off to boarding school." I gave him a shifty, sideways glance.

"She's not going anywhere," Appa said, grimly. "Not if I have anything to do with it." So, I was going to be stuck with Misha. She wasn't going anywhere anytime soon. Strangely, it didn't fill me with dread like I'd thought it would.

***

*Will you please pick up my call?*

That was the tenth message from Ashar that I'd ignored. Wouldn't it be easier to just block him? My finger hovered over his name. All I needed to do was tap. But I couldn't. Instead I put my phone on silent and pulled out a book to read.

There was a new Young Adult Fantasy that I'd been dying to read and I finally had time to get down to it. According to my father, I wasn't going to school tomorrow either. We were going to get back on the family track before we tackled the issue of school.

What was the family track exactly? Our family certainly didn't have a track. We were typical of Indian traffic. We darted around haphazardly, without any semblance of rules and crashed into each other with alarming results. As our debacle at the school had just established. If that wasn't a carwreck, I don't know what was.

Appa appeared at my door again. "Kitty, that boy is here again." Ashar. My father's sneer was reserved for him. I made my way down the stairs to find him standing in the narrow corridor, looking awkward and uncomfortable.

"What?" I asked.

"I wanted to talk to you," he said.

"I didn't want to talk to you. I thought that was obvious since I wasn't taking your calls."

Appa cleared his throat behind me.

"What?" I rounded on him.

"Manners," he said, mildly. "Would you like to come into the drawing room beta?"

Beta? Now he was Beta? What happened to 'that boy'?

"Thank you, Uncle." Ashar skirted me carefully and followed my father down the corridor and into the living area at the end of it. I followed mutinously and plonked myself in a chair across from them. The two of them chatted amicably about cricket and whether it was time for the captain to retire from captaincy.

I glowered at the two of them, my mind still on my last conversation with Ashar. Selfish, he'd called me. I hadn't forgotten. Nor had I forgotten that Misha was the one he liked.

"Are you here to meet Misha?" I asked, abruptly. "Because she's not here."

Aunty Sush had dragged her off for a counselling session. I hoped it worked. They really had a lot to work through.

"Why would I be here to meet Misha?" He looked startled.

Appa looked at the two of us and wisely decided to leave the room. He disappeared so fast, it was almost like magic.

"You mean other than the fact that you're in love with her?" I retorted.

"Did you hit your head on something?" he asked. "What the hell are you talking about? Why would I be in love with Misha? Who the hell told you rubbish like that?"

"You did!" I shouted. "Just before you called me selfish."

"You were being selfish." He got to his feet, angrily. "Misha was in trouble and you were obsessing about yourself."

It was amazing how much words could hurt. It felt like he had ripped my heart out and stomped all over it.

"Then why the hell are you here now?" I spat out. "Come back when your precious Misha is here."

Ashar groaned, scrubbing his hands through his hair. "You're as demented as your psycho sister."

"And you're as much of an ass as Samar is." I yelled back.

He froze. And for a moment, anger left me and I was scared. I had gone too far. "I had a crush on Misha a very long time ago," he said quietly, evenly. "I don't anymore. I came to check on you because I was worried about you."

He turned away and walked towards the door. I stayed frozen in place. Suddenly, he turned back and came to me. He stopped a few feet away and stared at me.

"I do like you, Katya. I didn't want to. I really didn't. After the way Misha hurt me, the last thing I needed was to be interested in her sister – step or otherwise. I tried to ignore you, insult you, annoy you … but in the end it was all of no use. I still ended up liking you. I really wish I didn't but I do."

And with those last damning words, he walked out of the door.

# Thirty

## Misha

"You won't believe what my daughter has done."

The therapist looked a little startled by my mother's outburst with no greeting of any sort in sight. This emergency counselling session my mother had scheduled was going to be a lot of work, for all of us.

"Why don't you both sit down?" She gestured to the chairs in front of her table. I sat. My mother didn't.

She was in full lawyer mode. She strode from one end of the tiny cabin to the other, arms waving and teeth clenching as she launched into a tirade of everything that had happened today.

I slumped lower in my seat as the now familiar fatigue took over. I tuned my mother out. There was nothing new in her rant that I needed to pay attention to. I sensed the therapist watching me as my mother continued to list all the ways in which I made her life a living hell. She was missing out a few points, I thought idly. Should I remind her?

"Mrs Banerjee." The therapist's firm voice finally cut her off. "Can you please sit down?"

My mother sat, panting from the exertion of spewing venom about her daughter.

"Misha, do you want to tell me what happened today?" She turned kind, caring eyes towards me. Was that a learned skill, I wondered dispassionately. It was highly unlikely that she truly cared.

"No." I shrugged. "She already covered all the highlights."

"Ask her," My mother hissed like a fire breathing dragon. "Ask her how that boy got a picture of her without any clothes."

Ahh, yes. That poisoned dart from Samar's family had found its rightful target.

"We were on a video call and he asked me to take my top off." I kept my eyes on the doctor. "I did."

My mother made a sound that was a lot like a pressure cooker releasing steam. Even the doctor looked startled.

"Mrs Banerjee, could you please wait outside? I'd like to speak to Misha alone."

My mother's entire body quivered with rage. I knew her well enough to know that she resented being kicked out but couldn't find it in her to defy the doctor's authority.

The door shut with a defiant thud a minute later.

"Well done," I told the doctor who was watching me. "You handled her very efficiently."

"I didn't handle her, Misha. I'm just doing my job. Now," she leaned forward. "Talk to me."

I wanted to. I really did but the words wouldn't come. So, I just slumped lower in my seat.

"You know what your mother just did? Asking how he got the picture in the first place? We call that victim blaming."

"And here I thought it was slut shaming," I murmured.

"That too," she said, with an appreciative smile. "I'm glad to see you're aware of things like that. I don't want you to let that seep into your head. I wouldn't want you to think like that."

"Does it matter?"

"Does what matter?" she asked. "What I think. It doesn't matter to anyone else. Why should it matter to me?"

"Is that how you feel?" She leaned forward, her pen tapping against her notepad.

I shrugged. "Are we done yet?"

"We're just getting started." She made a note on her pad. I tried to see what she'd written but it was tilted away from me.

"I don't really have anything to say." I shifted in my chair. "Can I go home please?"

"You can go home whenever you want to, Misha. You're not a prisoner here."

I shot to my feet. "Thank you. I'll see you then."

I had my hand on the doorknob when the counsellor's voice rang in my ears, "How do you feel about Samar now?"

My fingers clenched around the handle.

"I hate him." I glared at her over my shoulder. "Obviously."

She watched me with those fake kind and concerned eyes.

"What else am I supposed to feel?" I exploded, storming back into the room.

"You tell me," was all she said.

"He used me, betrayed me and destroyed me. I hate him and I hope he rots in hell." I didn't realise I had tears streaming down my face. "He was supposed to be the one person who loved me and now..."

My words trailed off as I stared at her, aghast at what I'd revealed.

"And now what?" she asked.

"Now there is no one who does." I collapsed into the chair with a low keening wail. She was around the desk with a box of tissues in a moment. She sat beside me in silence as I cried, poisonous, hurtful tears that burst from me like a dam had broken inside me.

And maybe it had. By the time I was done, there was nothing left inside of me.

And then we started to talk. By the end of the session, I was feeling a lot calmer and a lot more open to anything the counsellor had to say. Which was a good thing since she seemed to think I was both depressed and bulimic.

"Will I get better?" I asked.

"Yes, you will," she smiled at me. "You're going to not only get better but also feel better. We're going to work together to change your narrative. Craft one that works for you."

"Change my narrative?" I wanted to laugh. "Is that straight out of your psychology textbooks?"

"Yes. My translation of it is to tell the world to go to hell because you're in control of your life and your happiness. Not anybody else; not your parents, not Samar, not Mallika, not even Katya. Only you."

***

We drove home in silence. Whatever the therapist had told my mother while I waited in the reception had her darting anxious glances at me. I ignored her and stared out of the window. The car ride was mercifully short and we reached before either of us said something we'd regret later.

I'd just gotten out and slammed the car door shut when Ashar came storming out of our front door. My eyebrows shot up to my hairline as I saw him walk right past us without acknowledging us.

He made it to the gate before I saw his manners kick him in his ass. He took a deep breath, muttered something and came back to my mother.

"Good evening Aunty." He gave her his trademark glower.

"No, no, no." My mother backed away from him. "No more

boys. I don't want to see any more boys around the girls."

I almost laughed at both their expressions. Ma looked vengeful and Ashar horrified.

"What if either Katya and I decide we're lesbians or even bisexuals? Are you going to ban girls from meeting us too?"

"I am not in the mood for your attitude, Misha," she screeched. Ashar took a hasty step back.

I smiled and gave him a small wave. "Go," I mouthed. He nodded once and took off like his ass was on fire. I didn't blame him. If I had somewhere else to go, I would run too.

The door opened and Uncle Kannan appeared in the doorway.

"What is all that noise about?" he asked in his normal, genial voice. Ma just shook her head and pushed past him. I walked up and stopped a step beneath where he stood.

"How are you?" he asked, his eyes trying to study my face.

I wrapped my arms around him and hugged him tight.

"Thank you," I whispered. "I finally understand why Ma left Papa for you."

He stiffened, gently holding me away from him. "Misha…"

"I would have too, if I'd been in her place." I winked at him.

He blushed adorably and awkwardly patted me on my shoulders as I walked past him.

"I still don't know what you saw in her though," I said as I made my way down the corridor.

"Misha." He shook his head in reproof.

I laughed and looped my arm through his as we walked. "Okay. Okay. I'll behave."

"We need to talk," he said as we walked into the room where Ma sat on the couch and Katya stood in the corner looking for all the world like someone had shoved a poker up her ass.

Ma looked up when we came in, her glance taking in our looped arms. Something softened in her face as she watched us. Katya on the other hand stiffened up even more.

I sighed and removed my arm from Uncle Kannan's. I didn't blame Katya. He was too precious to share.

"We need to decide if we're filing a complaint with the police."

His words were like a dash of icy water. All three of us focused on him.

"Kannan, I don't think we should," Ma said. She looked as tired as I felt.

"Why not? Don't you think we should do right by Misha?"

"How is making this a public spectacle doing right by her?" Ma demanded, jumping up from the couch. "What about her future? What about her reputation?"

"My reputation?" I wanted to laugh but I thought it might push my mother over the edge. Although it looked like she might have taken that leap already.

"You don't talk." She whirled on me. "You've caused enough trouble already."

"Sush," Uncle Kannan rebuked her. "This is not her fault."

"Not her fault? Not her fault??"

Oh dear. Ma was probably going to shriek herself into a heart attack. "Okay. It's not entirely her fault." Uncle Kannan tried to pacify her.

"Listen," I started but nobody was listening to me.

Ma and Uncle Kannan were arguing and it looked like I might just be the reason for their impending divorce. Shouldn't that make me happy? And yet, strangely it didn't. I'd adjusted to this new reality of ours and I wasn't ready to trade it in.

"Why don't we ask Misha what she wants?" Katya's calm voice sliced through all the commotion.

The parentals turned towards me. "What do you want, Misha?" Uncle Kannan asked. Ma just stared daggers at me.

"I don't want to file a case," I said calmly. Ma's shoulders sagged with relief.

"Why?" Uncle Kannan asked.

"I want to put it behind me. I've done plenty of stupid stuff and now I just want to move on from the whole mess."

He nodded, understanding lightening his gaze.

"You finish out this school year and we'll move both of you to another school for your eleventh and twelfth grades. A new start is just what both of you need."

"Misha will be going to boarding school," Ma butted in. "Arun and I have already decided on that."

"No, she won't." Uncle Kannan held my gaze.

"Kannan don't interfere in this. Arun won't like it."

"I don't give a flying fuck what Arun would or wouldn't like. He is not the one living here parenting our children."

Katya gasped at his language and expression. I smiled at him in delight. This avatar of Uncle Kannan was absolutely wonderful.

Ma looked flabbergasted, like her life had taken a strange turn at some point and she couldn't find her way back.

"Tell Arun that it is our decision. As Misha's primary caregivers, we will decide what is best for her," he said. "If you want, I can speak to him."

But Ma was already shaking her head. "I'll tell him," she muttered. "We don't need any more drama in this house."

Katya walked up to me. "Do you have those texts that Samar sent you? The ones asking for," she glanced behind her at the parentals, but they were busy arguing with each other under their breath, "nudies and stuff," she whispered.

I nodded, warily. Why did she want to know?

"Let's go print them out along with the screenshots I took of his post. Oh, also, let's pull up stuff on when he made that video about you puking on him and print whatever we can."

"Why?"

"Ammunition," she said, briskly. "We'll make a file. That way we're ready for anything he comes up with."

I raised an eyebrow. "I'm assuming you have a file on me?"

"Of course," she smiled cheekily. "It's colour coded and filed alphabetically too."

"You are such a dork," I groaned.

We were almost to the door when Ma called out, "Misha, your father is on the phone. He wants to talk to you."

"No thanks," I said, meeting Uncle Kannan's eyes. "Tell him my father is right here and I've already spoken to him."

# Thirty-One

## Katya

The note appeared on my desk midway through our Hindi class. I stared at it, unwilling to open it. I didn't know what he wanted to say. I didn't care. Or so, I told myself.

I ignored it and went back to writing in my notebook. His hand appeared in the periphery of my vision and he shoved the note closer to me.

I shoved it back. It toppled over the side of my desk and landed near my feet.

Ashar glared at me. I returned the glare with equal ferocity. Luckily, the bell rang and class wrapped up. I shoved my books into my backpack and headed out to the cafeteria to meet Bhavya.

I didn't look back at Ashar. I didn't! Ok, let me be fair, maybe just a sneak peek. He had picked up the note and put it back on his table.

Lunch was a rather complicated affair with Bhavya and the other girls trying to get me to spill about what happened in the principal's office. It was a lot like playing dodgeball. I had to give them some details without saying anything truly important.

I envied Misha and her suspension. I'd left her lounging in bed with her headphones on. And here I was, dodging notes and awkward questions.

"So how long is Misha suspended for?"

"A week," I answered, biting into my sandwich so I didn't have to say anything more.

"Hi Katya."

I looked up to see Mallika, Misha's supposed best friend standing by our table. I choked on my sandwich and started to gasp and splutter.

Bhavya smacked me on my back hard enough to dislodge not just the sandwich but also what felt like my lungs.

"Thanks," I told her, my eyes watering. I moved out of range of her weaponized hands so she couldn't 'help' me anymore.

"Hi," I said to Mallika who was still standing there. I took a sip of water and waited for the burning sensation to subside.

"How is Misha?" she asked.

"Why don't you ask her?" I raised an eyebrow.

She shifted uncomfortably from one foot to the other. "I think she's blocked me."

The table went silent. Everyone was watching us now. Juicy gossip like this was not to be sneezed at.

"I don't know what you want me to do about it."

"Nothing," she mumbled. "I just wanted to know if she was okay."

"She is," I answered, abruptly. If Mallika was so worried about her friend, she wouldn't have turned on her the way she did.

"Could you tell her I asked?"

Ahh. That's what this was about. I was supposed to be the olive branch. No, thank you.

"Tell her yourself." I blurted out.

"I just told you she blocked me," she snapped.

“Then find a way to reach out to her. It’s not rocket science. A way that does not go via me,” I added when she opened her mouth to reply.

She shut her mouth, glared at me and stormed away.

Oh well. There goes our supposed budding friendship.

I was just biting into my sandwich again when someone else stopped at the table next to me. Now what? I raised my eyes and they met Ashar’s furious ones. “We need to talk.”

“I don’t want to talk to you,” I replied. “Is that so hard to understand?”

Our table of interested onlookers held their breath. I was providing them with enough entertainment to last a month at least. Ashar was about to say something when Coach Sebastian walked up to us.

“Ashar, we’re going to have the mixed team practice today. See that everyone is ready and waiting on the court at 5.”

Oh shit. “Sure Coach.” Ashar kept his eyes fixed on me. I refused to look away. “I’m looking forward to it.”

***

If there was a more bloodthirsty game of basketball, then I was yet to see it. Coach Sebastian had put us on opposite teams and we played like it was a National Championship match and we had everything at stake.

I dribbled the ball and made my way across the court keeping an eye out for Ashar who had a talent for sneaking up on me. Dodging past Karthik, I got ready to shoot when the ball was spun out of my hand.

I whirled around ready to spit fire at Ashar only to find Akrithi speeding away from me. Disgruntled, I ran to catch up only to see her pass the ball to Ashar who scored. Disgusted with myself for losing the point and with him for tag teaming me like that, I ran to take my place again.

"Go Kitty!"

My brain took a minute to catch up to what I'd heard. Adrenalin still pumping from the game, I turned to face my heckler.

Misha grinned at me, her hands still cupped around her mouth as she yelled again, "Kitty! Kitttyyy!"

My mouth fell open. She was wearing ripped jeans and a pink tank top that screamed for attention amidst the rest of us sweaty mortals in our dusty uniforms.

Coach called for a break and I jogged over to her.

"What are you doing here?"

She put her hands on her hips and tossed her hair back.

"Haven't you missed me?"

I grinned. Strangely enough I had. What was school without your evil stepsister's shadow looming over everything?

"I'm just coming from another emergency counselling session. My therapist said," she continued, dropping her pose. "That I should own my narrative, my story. She's teaching me how to do it and I'm starting with my first steps today."

"Own your story?" I repeated, bemused.

"Make it my own. I've been handing over control to Ma, Papa, Samar … everyone but the person who should be writing it … me!"

"That sounds…" I considered the idea a bit more. "Pretty fabulous. But are you allowed to be here when you're suspended?"

She rolled her eyes at me. "What is with you? Do rules turn you on or something?"

I shook my head. "You're certainly owning your narrative."

She laughed. "Come on Kitty. You should do the same."

"Do what?" Coach was calling the players back onto the field. I needed to go.

"Be you. Be Kitty."

I looked at her grinning at me. My arch nemesis; perpetual thorn in my side, pain in the neck sister.

Be Kitty. No more trying to fit in. No more trying to be anyone other than who I was. No more keeping quiet when I wanted to scream. *Be Kitty*. Write my own story.

"We're going to be fine, Kitty Cat," Misha said, her normally feral grin becoming gentler.

I nodded and smiled back. Yes. Yes, we were.

I ran back to the court and bumped straight into Ashar. He backed up a step when he saw me coming right at him.

"Do you like me?" I asked.

"Yes," he said, his wary gaze going from Misha to me. "Are you going to hit me?"

"Not right now. Do you like me, Ashar? Not as a friend? But as something more?"

He dropped the basketball he was holding. "Yes, you idiot. That's what I've been trying to tell you all along. But you won't stop yelling at me long enough to listen."

I smacked his arm. "Calling me an idiot is not romantic."

"I never said I was romantic." He scowled at me, rubbing his arm. I picked up the basketball he'd dropped.

"See you on the court, Captain. I'm going to destroy you."

His smile was slow to come but when it did, it was worth everything. Writing my own story was wonderful indeed. And being Kitty was everything.

***

# Acknowledgements

To say I stand on the shoulders of giants is nothing but an understatement as I would be unable to get through even a second of this life without the unconditional support and love of my family. To Dad, Mom, Rohit and Aisha, you guys are my giants.

To Mishka – my Misha and Katya both, thank you for being you and for inspiring me to write this book. And finally, to Zoe, my love, and the largest portion of my heart, you my darling, are truly the best of me. It's my privilege to be your mother.

To Andaleeb, Apeksha and Debdatta – my writing tribe – a big thank you for always supporting me with constructive feedback, endless critiques and depthless friendship.

Crafted with passion and dedication, Hey Kitty is a project close to my heart, made possible by the collaborative efforts of remarkable individuals. I extend my heartfelt gratitude to Ajay Mago, publisher, Om Books International, and Shantanu Ray Chaudhuri, editor-in-chief, whose belief in the story ensured its journey to the hands of readers. Dr. Kirti Pathak, senior editor (children's division), your trust in this tale is truly appreciated. Arushi Barathi, editor, and Papiya Saha Singha, artist, thank you for your invaluable contributions in shaping this book. Last but certainly not the least, Sheela Roy, my editor, thank you for your unwavering support and infectious enthusiasm towards making *Hey Kitty* come alive.

# About the Author

A mother to a pre-teen and an aunt to a teenager, Shilpa Suraj often found herself floundering while trying to find the balance between being the 'cool' adult and the 'responsible' one. A published romance author with Harlequin, Mills & Boon India, Rupa Publications, Juggernaut and Storytel, Shilpa's notable successes include *Wrong, Married in Hate, Once Upon a Scandal* and *Rescued by Love* amongst others. She first forayed into children's writing with her contribution to the *Flipped Anthology: Mystery Stories / Sci-Fi Stories* by Harper Collins. Inspired by her travails in trying to be this generation's version of a cool parental figure, she sat down to pen her first Young Adult novel, the one in your hands now, *Hey Kitty*.